BEHIND THE LINE

An Enigma To Reveal

SYED MUSHARAF

BLUEROSE PUBLISHERS
India | U.K.

Copyright © Syed Musharaf 2024

All rights reserved by author. No part of this publication may be reproduced, stored in a retrieval system or transmitted in any form or by any means, electronic, mechanical, photocopying, recording or otherwise, without the prior permission of the author. Although every precaution has been taken to verify the accuracy of the information contained herein, the publisher assume no responsibility for any errors or omissions. No liability is assumed for damages that may result from the use of information contained within.

BlueRose Publishers takes no responsibility for any damages, losses, or liabilities that may arise from the use or misuse of the information, products, or services provided in this publication.

For permissions requests or inquiries regarding this publication, please contact:

BLUEROSE PUBLISHERS
www.BlueRoseONE.com
info@bluerosepublishers.com
+91 8882 898 898
+4407342408967

ISBN: 978-93-6452-627-2

Cover design: Tahira
Typesetting: Tanya Raj Upadhyay

First Edition: October 2024

FOREWORD

It is with immense pleasure that I introduce you to "Behind The Line" the debut novel by Syed Musharaf, a rising talent hailing from the idyllic Brakpora village in Anantnag District, India. Musharaf's love affair with literature began in his formative years, blossoming from a spark ignited in the heart of a curious fourth-grader. This passion has propelled him forward, etching his name amongst the winners of the prestigious NoticeBard National Essay Writing Competition not once, but twice. His literary prowess has further garnered recognition in the esteemed 'F For Fame' class of Weebly.com, a testament to his exceptional writing skills.

"Behind The Line" marks Musharaf's foray into the world of novel writing, and from the very first page, it is evident that a master storyteller is at the helm. This gripping drama-thriller promises to take you on a thrilling ride, where the lines between reality and deception blur. Musharaf's adept use of language and his profound understanding of human emotions weave a captivating narrative that will leave you enthralled until the very last sentence.

Prepare to be transported to a world where suspense hangs thick in the air, and secrets lurk in the shadows. "Behind The Line" is a must-read for anyone who enjoys a good dose of drama and intrigue. It is a compelling debut that showcases the immense potential of this talented author. I urge you to delve into this captivating story and experience the magic of this wonderful author's words for yourself.

TABLE OF CONTENTS

1. A FRESH START TO A NEW BEGIN… 1
2. A DEADLY GIFT… 9
3. I AM YOUR WELLWISHER..! 12
4. NO BIG DEAL! 17
5. MANY QUESTIONS, MANY TROUBLES. 23
6. A ROBBERY FOR GOOD… I GUESS 29
7. WELCOME TO THE GAME....................................35
8. IT HAS OVERTURNED KAZUO..! 40
9. THE FIRST AND LAST CHANCE...........................44
10. GOING BACK WHERE IT STARTED..! 49
11. BACK TO NORMAL… 55
12. MY MOM…THE BEST ADVISOR 60
13. MEETING IN NAPERVILLE… 65
14. FARTHER I GO, THE NEARER I COME 72
15. WHY ONLY I LOST EVERYTHING? 78
16. SURPRISINGLY BACK 84
17. A FRIEND INDEED 90
18. LESSON LEARNT; DON'T TRY TO BE A HERO! 98
19. ENIGMA REVEALED!...105

1. A FRESH START TO A NEW BEGIN...

The morning light filled my room. Sparrows were sitting in a queue on an electric wire and singing tunes. A new day, a new life had just started. Mom rushed in my room with a mug of coffee in her right hand and a newspaper in her left one. She placed the coffee on my side-table and leaned the newspaper towards me saying, "Look at the job offer on the top-left side. I guess this one will work!" Everyday my mother used to introduce new job offers to me and I used to refuse them. How can a 17 year old boy like me get a job when he is not even qualified as an adult? Still whenever I used to, I refused very politely because the death of my father had already affected her a lot. She was working at an ELECTRONIC GOODS store and hence the salary was moderate. Most of the days passed peacefully but sometimes we were hard up. "Do you really believe this one will work?" I said, taunting her. "Listen Kazuo, you know how hard we are with money sometimes. Let's insure each and every thing!" she said desperately. "I know Mom and I am also trying to find an opportunity from which I could earn" I lied. I used to tell her this every time but I never used to execute it. "So please find yourself a part-time a job" she said, debating. "I am not an adult yet, I still have my studies left! How the hell on Earth will I concentrate on them?" I argued back which I shouldn't have done. As expected, the argument continued for over an hour until it was time for school. "Mom, I am going to be late!" I cried. My bus used to arrive at my place at 8:00 AM. I was always late in waking up but however I always managed it to the time as well. As usual, my bus had arrived and I was late by 3 minutes. I waved a goodbye to Mom and she planted a kiss on my cheek. I, in return also kissed her and after a goodbye of two minutes, the bus left my stop. Everyone, including the bus driver, gave a dirty look to me. They were irritated with all this which they called 'A weird affection' because according to them, 'TWO' minutes was a lot of their time. But also, how long could I defend this statement. This was the way I loved living, with my mother. I had the responsibilities of a son as well as that of a husband, though I wasn't working. But a husband is not only the one who keeps on earning. He also needs to understand the psyche of his family in every situation and manage them. My father couldn't so he left us on our own. Still, I never considered that his mistake. He suffered from some serious flu in the late weeks of September when I was only 7 years old and after that internal pain took over his body for a long time, he didn't have the patience left anymore.

On reaching to school, I started revising some Mathematical equations and formulas. I just walked 15 meters and then received a punch right on spot. It felt like a thousand needles getting pricked into my nose and it simply burned out all the mathematical operations from my brain. Steve, the gangster of our school was there, standing right in front of me. Though everyone in the school had some irritation with me, Steve conquered them all in this matter. He hated me from the very beginning and every time, tried to push me to the limits. I, somehow, always managed the situation doing nothing. "How are you Mr. Weirdo? Oh sorry! You might not be ok after that!" he teased me and his whole gang burst into laughter, a scary one! I was never able to figure out why everyone in the school considered me as weird…My dress-up was same as theirs. I had two eyes, two ears, a pair of legs and that one of arms also. Everything was intact, except one thing. I had no social bonding with anyone. There were only a few of the students who replied to my greetings and barely smiled at me. I had only one lad by my side, forever, and he came to my rescue every time I fell into something terrible. Hearing this fresh encounter with Steve from a boy, Zhen, my best friend rushed to the scenario. Seeing him, Steve and his gang ran in fear because he was a very huge guy. We were long time friends, almost from 7 years and I knew him better than anyone. He lived alone in a big bungalow along with his pet dog Rogers. Nobody knew where he came from or who his parents were, but in our first meeting, we patched up as good friends. He was my one year senior, really bizarre from all the sides, including his left hand. It neither had five fingers nor even six. He had seven large, extra boned and webbed fingers. I sometimes even saw him using them. While writing, punching someone or during his extra-class of judo training. "Hey Kazuo! Are you ok?" he asked. "Don't worry...I am ok" I replied. "No, you are not, I will teach these goons a lesson later during the recess!" he said, his tone a bit angry. "Don't worry Zhen, I am ok. I need not to mind these foolish steps by someone!" I said like a big man talking. "I am definitely not going to tolerate this Kazuo, I am going to..." "Listen Zhen, I know that you always try to be a messiah for me but don't you think that I shouldn't mind these steps by someone who thinks that he can humiliate me using such dirty tricks?" I interrupted him in his mid sentence. "If you think so, then I forgive them this time. Also, Mr. Arthur will be showing us the copy of the Murcaxro, the extraordinary painting and do you know what? We will be visiting the museum really soon!" I would never believe Zhen unless I get a strong proof of what he was saying. "That's great! But I've never heard of the Murcaxro. What is that?" I replied. "Dude, it's one of the most precious things in our city, some 20 years old only! I wish I could have it hanging on my lobby wall!" he replied, talking nonsense only. "Zhen, the dirty walls won't support it, you know..." I said, making him realize how bad he was at hygiene management. "Oh yes, thank God I remember! Come to the cafeteria in the recess, I need to tell you something" he said. "What's it? Tell me?" I inquired. "I'll tell you there only" he replied.

In our first period, our teacher Mr. Arthur showed us a painting of a beautiful girl playing a flute. "Look children, this is a copy of the painting Murcaxro and I got the permission from the museum officials to show you this. We would also be visiting the State Museum next week on Wednesday to take a look at the master pieces there" Mr. Arthur informed. So Zhen was right. I also decided to have a look because I wanted to feel fresh but if Steve would be around then the situation won't be same. I would always feel like a rotten apple which could be smashed anytime with a big boot and I don't want Steve to be that.

In the recess time I went to meet Zhen in the cafeteria. "Hey, come on tell me. What is it?" I asked him. "Yup buddy, you're here. Well Kazuo, I was thinking of cleaning the attic today. Can you please help?" he replied. "Yes, why not! I'll keep my bag and come to your place" I replied back. "Why to keep your bag first at home. You can directly come to my place. We can have some fresh apple pie also first" he said. "Well, shouldn't I inform Mom first" I said in a warning tone. "Alright, that seems to be fine to me. Go home first and inform your 'dear' Mom!" he taunted. "Not again Zhen. I am not a 'Mamma's boy' now" I replied and we both laughed loud. The school hours went dim and dim until the afternoon Sun showed up and the bell rang to let us go. I rushed to my bus and Zhen cried behind, "Kazuo, remember your promise? I won't be able to clean it up alone!" To be honest I had no idea about that promise after surviving my classes. Still, I replied, "Of course buddy. I got your back!" I reached home as quiet as my bus. Mom was on the couch, having rest. "Wake up Mom. I need to tell you something!" I whispered so that she won't get angry. Waking up my Mom during her sleep was like putting hands in a snake's cave. "Oh dear, you're back. What do you want to tell?" she asked, her eyes still closed. "Zhen invited me to his home for the cleanup of his attic. I think I should go!" I told her. "Ok, go but be home soon or you know the consequences!" she replied. "Not better than anyone!" I replied back, kissed her on the forehead and left. It took me almost 15 minutes by brisk, foot walk to reach Zhen's place. The beautiful bungalow had lost its beauty as Zhen was the owner. He was a very lazy but still dependable guy. All mattered was what the situation was. "I am here dude. Where are you?" I cried just as I entered. "Up here...Please come up here!" he cried and then coughed. I reached to the dirtier attic and unexpectedly, Zhen had already started the cleaning. "What the hell buddy! That looks messy!" I said as he saw me. "Stop complaining, wear that apron right there and start from cleaning that wooden trunk. The mop is waiting for your dry hands" he replied and laughed alone. "Dude, I am not cleaning that crap! I mean just look at that!" I said, after watching it all covered in dust and spider-webs. "Man, you want to help or not?" he asked irritatingly. "Ok, ok...I am cleaning that. Don't talk like that, huh" I replied, trying to be a savage. With a heavy stone on my heart, I cleaned the trunk from the outside first and then opened it. As I was cleaning the inside of it, I saw something very unfamiliar to my eyes. It was a phone. "Zhen, what is this?" I asked as I lifted the scary thing in my hand. "What? Oh a phone! How did that land up in here?" he replied. "That's what I am asking you. How did you get that?" I asked him. "Dude, this trunk is not mine! It used to be Dad's. Maybe, this phone is also his!" he replied. There was a sense of doubt in his tone. "So, what should we do with this? It doesn't look too messed up either!" I asked him. "Take it with yourself" he replied with ease. "Shut up. Mom will tear me into a hundred pieces!" I replied. "No that's a good idea! You have it and leave, I will clean the rest myself" he said, pushing me out. "Dude, listen to me!" I kept saying the same sentence until the door steps. "You might be tired. I will get the pie tomorrow for you in the school. I promise!" Zhen said stammering. "Ah, ok!" I replied as he closed the door behind. I kept watching the phone for 5 minutes until I questioned myself why I accepted this from Zhen? Why?! There was something doubtful in this moment. Zhen never acts like this but today he was stammering. He broke out in sweat while talking to me about this garbage which was of no use for me other than help me in getting a thrash from Mom. Finally, I started walking back home.

I push open the door of our apartment. I held the thing tight in my pocket. "Hey darling...Are you tired? Should I bring in some eatables for you?" Mom asked just as I entered. "N-n-n-o-o-o Mom, I am not having any appetite!" I replied. She paused for a while and then said again, "Are you ok Kazuo? You are shivering!" She inquired. "No! I am good... Just have a look at me!" I said. Oops! The wrong thing said. I was really shivering and my legs were stiffened. Holding the phone tightly in my pocket, I entered my room, avoiding any eye contact with Mom. She stared me until I closed the door and I knew what would happen next. I hooked my sweater into the hanger, released my tie to my belly so that I could breath and closed my eyes for 10 seconds. I was feeling much better, but not for too long.

2. A DEADLY GIFT...

I was sitting quietly on my chair, thinking what would happen if Mom got to know about 'THIS THING' which could become my shroud. KNOCK!!! "Kazuo...Kazuo...Are you ok son?" Mom asked in voice of suspicion. "I am ok Mom...No need to worry!" I replied. There was a silence for a minute until Mom roared, "Open the door Kazuo...NOW!" "Yes Mom...Opening!" I replied as fast as possible and tried to find a place to hide the phone. My Mom was aware of every corner of our flat but still I managed to find a place above my Book-Shelf to hide this crap. "Yes Mom..." I asked after opening the door. "What took you so long? I am afraid that you aren't feeling well" Mom replied. "No...I am good Zhen" I said whatever came out of my mouth. "What?" Mom said surprisingly. "Sorry...I meant Mom!" I replied with a fake giggle. "I can never understand you. Ok, come with me... I have an appointment with a doctor" she said and I thanked God, thinking that her attention was diverted from my shivering. "You go...I'll pay a visit to the washroom" I said to her. "Ok" she replied in short. I closed the door again and then plugged in the charger of my Mom's mobile phone into the phone. BEEEP...REBOOT. The voice came from the phone and it showed a sign. Yes! It was working...! Now I could return it to Zhen and he won't be having any sort of excuses like 'IT ISN'T WORKING OR IT IS NOT THE SAME'. I opened the door again and then called Mom who was busy doing her Make-up, a thing that I never stopped her from doing. It was because I only wanted her attention to stay away from Dad's death and the best way to do so was only by letting her do the things she loved to. Otherwise I was very strict with my responsibilities as a son. I again called Mom in a bit louder voice than before, "MOM!" "Yes!" she exclaimed, shouting louder than me. "Do you want us to be late?" I said, trying to be a bit over-smart. "Coming in 2 minutes!" she replied. After her 2 minutes which were actually 45 minutes of the real world, she came rushing down the stairs and told me to quickly wear the shoes and take the keys. I hated this part, not only for my Mom but for everyone. First you are yourself the reason for something late and then scold others like they are it. I got the keys from the key holder and then locked the door of our flat. We lived on the first floor of an unknown building in some god-damn unknown streets of Chicago. Mom again cried, "You want to come or not?" "Coming Mom!" I cried back. We walked to my bus-stop and then waited for a cab. After 5 minutes, a cab arrived. I sat quietly at the back-seat and my Mom at the front. She started talking with the cab driver which was as usual. In the sense, I meant that whenever I and Mom booked a cab, she always used to talk with the drivers, asking each and everything, in brief, about their whole life. Even after all of this, I never dared to tell her that 'You ask things to gain knowledge, not to make someone fall from knowledge'

The thoughts of the phone were still revolving in my head. I had already decided to give it back to Zhen tomorrow. After sometime, we were at the clinic of Dr. Augitali, an Egyptian Orthopedician. I, in my childhood was often made to visit him by my father because of a swollen toe in my right foot. Therefore, he was having close relationships with my father and was having the same with me and my Mom too. We visited inside and my mother started talking with him also as usual. I was shocked that she wasn't tired, even after talking with the cab driver for over 20 minutes. After the doctor was done with his work, I tried to quickly rush out of the clinic because I was super tired and this tiredness was spreading over my whole body like poison. We returned late at night. We had our dinner outside and now weren't having any appetite. I went straight into my room and checked the phone. It was fully charged. I kept it on the table and smiled at it. I wanted it to consider this smile a farewell. My eyes became heavier and heavier until I wasn't aware that I fell in a very deep sleep.

3. I AM YOUR WELLWISHER...!

My alarm clock ringed at 6:30 AM as usual. My morning schedule followed as usual. I left for the Bus stop as usual. The mobile phone was in my left pocket unusually. I sat in the bus and took the corner seat, right against the window. The bus moved and I felt a little buzz in my left pocket. I didn't pay much attention to it. After sometime the same pocket buzzed again. I thought that it was the phone. On reaching to school, I directly went into the restroom and checked it. 2 missed calls from a same phone number. How is it possible to receive calls and that too from a same phone number? Does it mean that there is a nanokey also in this phone? I checked and found a single, black colored, pre-attached key, only eligible for calling. Still in shock, I went out of the restroom and received a punch with a knotted fist right on my face. My reflex was very quick but only in remembering that I had received the same on my nose yesterday and day before yesterday. Actually every day. Again Steve was standing there with his gang. Without uttering a single word, they started to laugh again but this time not a scary one but a STUPID one! Zhen wasn't available on the spot and thus for my good, I walked out of the corridor without saying anything. The phone was still in my hands and I started hating this thing now. I noticed that I had blood pouring out of my nose. I tried to call the person back but it didn't go as expected. I was really confused and had millions of thoughts running in my head. I started searching for Zhen but wasn't able to find him. On asking to his classmates, I came to know that he was absent. How lucky I really was! I had to hide this from Mom for another day. BUZZZZ! BUZZZZ! The voice came from the phone. It was a call from the same number. I picked it up. "Hello! Am I talking to Kazuo Tanaka?" the voice said first. My tongue locked up and my eyes spread like fungus. Somehow, I dared to talk. "Yes sir, but may I know who is talking" I replied. "I am one of your father's friends" he said. The thoughts that were coming in my mind were intrigue. How this man called specifically only me, how he can call on this number which has no identity of its own, how Zhen got this damned thing and how this guy knew my father? Curiosity took over my confusion. The only one who could answer these very questions was Zhen himself. In confusion, I disconnected the call. He called me 37 times that day and finally, during recess; I used my brain and switched the phone off. During the evening time, I was out with Maxwell and Tony, the two sons of our next door neighbor. On returning, I again switched on the phone and checked that I had received some more 44 calls from the same number. The confusion inside me was slowly getting converted to fear. I thought of complaining this to the Police but what will I tell them? Will they ever believe me? I thought of picking up the call next time if he called and he called the same moment. "Hello Kazuo! Why weren't you picking up the phone" he said first. "Sir I don't know you and I will be getting a severe beating if Mom catches the hold of this phone. How you called me only...I just got this phone some 36 hours back and even nobody knows that. Can I please know who you are?" I said in a single breath. He replied with a laugh, "I am your Well-wisher son!" "What?" I asked in clear confusion again. "Don't be scared son. I will explain everything but first, please meet me" he replied. "Okay sir. Where should I meet you?" I asked again. "Be on the line...I will direct you" he said. I agreed and started to move quietly out of my room. Luckily, Mom was sleeping and therefore it didn't take me many efforts in hiding the phone from her today. I opened our main door and giant winds were blowing. I talked to the person again and asked, "Ok I am out. Where I've to go now?" "Move straight downstairs and keep walking. Now stop and walk from the left side until you see a small lane" he continued to direct me. I did the same and after some 5 minutes, I was at the end of a small lane. It felt like I was unfamiliar with this one. I was aware about every small or big street in our locality. While playing marbles or hide and seek with my kinder garden friends. While hiding from Mom when she was looking for me after coming to know about my performance in Mathematics. Or while I will rarely do some odd jobs of the market and take short cuts but I never saw this lane. I checked inside from the very end and found no body. I started searching for the man though I had never seen him. "Whom are you searching for Kazuo?" the voice came from my back. I looked back and a tall man with a long, warm and brown coat was half seated on the edge of a Bio-Degradable dustbin. He was wearing a black hat and was having a long ponytail of brown color. His eyes were light brown and he was wearing a brown mask also. I finally decided that he loved the color brown therefore his pants and long boots were also brown. I could see a little inside the boots, brown colored socks. I started stepping back in fear. "Hey why are you scared? Because of my looks?" he asked on seeing me stepping back every second. "Ah! No sir! But can I know who you are?" I asked hesitatingly. "Well! I am Dean Denbrough and I was your father's closest friend and business partner!" he replied. "What? But my Dad is long gone. I think you've mistaken me for someone else" I corrected him. "No son, I know everything! His sudden death shook me up but now it was no time left to regret then. His death had no impact on his business. We received the final due just 2 months after his death. His total share left was 5 million and because you are his son and heir to that property, I have to give you that, you understand?" he replied back. "But sir I have some questions to ask like how you called on this phone, how you know me and my father and most importantly, how you specifically called only me? I mean I have got this thing just few hours back and haven't used it. My friend Zhen gifted me this!" I asked him in a single breath. This thing has become my routine now but I can't do anything in that because I was totally confused, curious and scared. "Don't worry son...Cool down first of all and then we'll talk about these things and your friend as well!" he replied with generosity. "Alright then. When that share will be given to me?" I asked, trying to tackle his earlier statement. I don't think this will be a scam or something as this was not a coincidence as well. I have a lot to settle down with Zhen also. I was really angry. "Soon, but…. there is one thing!" he said. "What's that?" I inquired. "It is a thing that your father wanted me to have for him. He was waiting long for me to give him that and now, that he has left for the heavens, I want you to do that for him!" he replied. "Anything for Dad… What is it" I inquired questions upon questions because I thought I could trust Mr. Dean. He looked sober and he spoke sober and I could see that gentle love he had for my Dad in his eyes. "It's the Murcaxro!" It was the same painting that Mr. Arthur had showed us in the school.

4. NO BIG DEAL!

"But why did my Dad want something like that?" I asked. "It is because Murcaxro is made by your Dad and he had defeated a 'going to be a masterpiece' of a master painter through it! I don't remember his name now. The Murcaxro was given due respect and preserved in the State Museum and when your Dad was on the death-bed, his last wish was having the Murcaxro either hung on our office wall or it's income value given to your family after selling it!" he replied, tears in his eyes. What? Dad painted one of the most precious paintings of all time and I had no idea about it? I mean, I knew he was having some of his interest in arts but this here, was surreal! And if Mr. Dean was believed, that's why the Murcaxro has no signature of its painter on it as it was painted by Dad and that's also the reason why nobody is aware of its painter. I know Dad would never know let anyone know his identity. That was his nature and this here was a fact. I don't know why but my heart went heavy on my brain and instead of doubting him, I felt pity on him. I suppressed all my curiosity and fear. I finally put up all my courage and said, "Ok sir…Although I didn't know that my Dad was being indulged in something like painting, still I will help you but how?" "You need to help me and my two friends in a robbery!" he said. "What!"I exclaimed. "Yes, you heard it right" he replied like it was no big thing. "Don't worry Kazuo...Nothing will happen. The painting has a value worth 5 million dollars in the international market. It's yours by all rights. Won't you help your uncle? Ok, fine; won't you help me for your Dad?" he replied with ease. He saying 'Won't you help me for your Dad' hit me right on my sentiments. Also I remember how hard we were with our finance, so if this really helped, then I was ready. Finally, without any further conversation, I agreed to help Mr. Dean. "So, what is the plan?" I inquired. "I will tell you tomorrow evening right here...We'll talk about it" he replied.

I returned home late and went straight in my room. Mom was sleeping. I had whispered in her ear that we were having some assignments from our school project and that's why we fixed the meeting at Zhen's house. It was now no big deal to me, telling lies to her. I pulled out the phone from my back pocket. Seriously, it looked very innocent but it was really a Devil. My life was going to change because of it. I looked at the hanging picture in my room of Me, Dad and Mom. Tears ran down my face, I don't know why. Maybe because I was missing Dad or someone talked about him after years. All those questions about the phone call I received from Mr. Dean were dead now. I cancelled all my plans of giving this phone back to Zhen. I went straight in my bed, wiped off the tears and went to sleep.

Next morning, the sky was cloudy, it felt like all the sparrows in the world were dead and even Mom didn't woke up. I went in my room and she waved me a hello. I went close to her and said, "Good morning Mom. What happened? You don't seem well!" she opened her mouth a bit and said, "Oh darling! I am feeling a severe attack of fever. I think you should take a leave from school today." "Ok Mom let me prepare your breakfast." I replied. "Ok dear, I love you!" she said as I moved towards the kitchen. After having the breakfast, I washed up the dishes. I decided to take Mom to a doctor but she didn't agree. Mr. Dean had told me to reach the same place, the unknown lane by 5:30 PM. While I was preparing breakfast for us, the phone rang in pocket. The irritation I felt was just like a boiled potato, ready to be mashed. I wanted to kick it to pieces but I was compelled. "Kazuo, are you done?" Mom asked from behind. I was about to jump out of my skin when Mom again asked, "Kazuo, are you ok?" she said patting my shoulder and added, "I don't think that you should be out of bed today." "No Mom, I am good. There is nothing to worry about" I replied. "I have been noticing that your behavior these days hasn't been that acceptable. I hope all is fine" she inquired. "Mom, you don't need to worry about my behavior. I am good" I lied again. "Just do me a favor. Go in your bed and rest, please" she asked. My eyes went heavy, I thought it was because of the nightmares I got but I confirmed myself wrong when two streams of tears went down my eyes. "Hey, what happened dear?" she asked with fear. I hugged her and thought, 'Should I tell her why?' "Kazuo...Kazuo...LOOK AT ME!" Mom exclaimed. I tried not to make eye contact with her but she grabbed my face in her hands and said again, "I don't know what is wrong with you but I don't want you to be sad. Anything that strikes you, I am here!" she said and hugged me again. "Mom, it has been a lot of what we have gone through and I know that you miss Dad" I said and questioned myself that why I did? "Your Dad tried too hard my son but he couldn't bear. Talking about me, missing him, so I don't because I see all his good reflection in you" she replied emotionally and then added, "So now I know why you were crying, because you miss Dad, right?" "Mom, after Dad left, I promised many things to myself including not lying or deceiving you in any way. So please, forgive me but I have taken up a very serious step." I said. "What's it dear? Tell me" she asked with a smell of nervousness in her breath. I patted my heart and narrated the whole story that left her shocked. "So Mom, what do you say? Should we live a simple and usual life we already are in or will you allow me to help Mr. Dean?" I asked her. Before she could answer, her voice became pitched and her face turned red, almost purple. She collapsed on the stew, I made for breakfast and I didn't knew what to do? It was for sure that she didn't listen any of the things I said. I cried and soon, neither I was in my senses nor Mom. I felt my eyelids heavy, like bricks. I was about to lose my sense of consciousness and fell to the floor. Before something terrible could happen, I saw Mr. Dean opening up the door and lifting my Mom and me to his car downstairs. "Mr. Dean, what are you doing here, how you came to know about my house and why are…?" "Quiet dear! I will explain everything but first let's take her to the hospital!" he said interrupting me. I don't know how he got to know about my home and how he could be so punctual to this incident. Maybe he was spying on me or maybe he just came to give me a look or maybe he was just taking a walk through our dark-filled, narrow and smelly lanes. But I questioned myself, 'HOW HE CAME TO KNOW ABOUT MY ADDRESS!' There was something really fishy about this and for the first time in years, our well-made, decorated and simple living was disturbed, by finance as well as Mr. Dean. I don't know why but I was very vexed with him. I started to curse and bad-mouth him but then I came to my senses and questioned myself, 'What has he done that I am abusing him?' In fact he was the one who helped me in this harsh and troubled time. I have to correct myself and say what is actually right. The right thing was that I was the cause for this episode, I was the one who made Mom cry, I was the one who tensed and frustrated her and I was the one because of whom she was going to die before reaching the Hospital. A board showed; HOSPITAL 5 KMS AWAY and now I lost my full hope. I felt a sensation of burning from the inside and every time I breathed out, it felt like I was blowing flames. I decided that these were the last ones of mine. I closed my eyes and I could see Dad slapping me on the right side and Mom slapping on the left. And now the last thing I remember was me crying, Mom breathing heavily and Mr. Dean trying his best to reach the hospital as quickly as possible.

5. MANY QUESTIONS, MANY TROUBLES.

I tried not to fall unconscious before reaching, either the hospital or the coffin. Mr. Dean was driving at a speed of 10,000 km/hr which I noticed when the car was about to jump from the road as a roadblock was very near. Mr. Dean smashed the car through the block and kept on driving as it really didn't matter about his expensive looking car. I tried to have a look at Mom; if she still was breathing but the speed was as such that I wasn't able to. With the help of my good eyes, 10 second later, I could see the Hospital, 5 seconds later, I could see the Hospital gate, 3 seconds later I could see the Watchman and 1.23 seconds later I could see death in the face of a truck about to collide with our car. Mr. Dean gave a sudden brake, which actually wasn't a smart move as the truck came nearer. Before the collision could occur and I, Mom and Mr. Dean turn to ashes, the truck driver himself stopped his vehicle with an unexpected brake. With vexed and cruel eyes, he came out of the truck, opened the door of our car and got Mr. Dean from his collar. He punched him on his nose just like Steve used to punch me. A great World War III took place on the road between him and the driver but to my surprise, Mr. Dean wasn't beating or blowing him back. It's because of all this, I forgot about Mom. I crawled to the front seat and it felt like I was breathing air which consisted nails and screws. With all of my energy, I screamed and the people who were enjoying the driver hitting and kicking Mr. Dean, came and started getting me and Mom out of the car and into the hospital. The nurses came and on watching me covered in red colored skin, they immediately arranged a stretcher. On lying on it, it felt like all my bones were broken. I imagined if Mom was alive or... The male nurses got me and Mom to the 2nd floor and the doctors directed them to take us to the ICU. The tense look on their faces made me realize that I was not going to survive. I don't know what the doctors were talking or why they were screaming for Oxygen Cylinders. Lastly, I noticed my eyes closing and me finally crying out for Mom.

I slowly opened my eyes and saw a Glucose bottle hooked on a stand. An Oxygen Cylinder, which showed that it was about to end and some stitches on the left side of my chest. I watched the broken roof of the room for at least 15-20 minutes until I finally cried out loud, "Excuse me, anyone present around?" I suffered pain on my left side. After 7 more cries a nurse came and behind her came a doctor. I tried to get up from the bed and said, "Sir what sort of stitches are they, a surgery?" The doctor replied "Don't get up son, just lay and have some rest. You just had a slight panic attack and we had to treat it through fluid medication, nothing else. We have resolved it!" "Sir, my Mom was also there, is she ok?" I asked with a breath of tension. "Oh, she is, just unconscious but will come to senses in an hour or two" he replied. "But sir…what was wrong with her? All I remember was me talking to her and then she collapsed on the table." I asked. "She had a slight reflex of paralysis but there is nothing to worry about now" the doctor replied immediately. "How long do we need to stay here?" I asked. "Not for too long. It might seem scary but the stitches are only there because we had to inject some fluid medications in. Now have some rest!" he replied and left me alone with the nurse, who was busy reading a magazine. Everything in my life had suddenly changed and now I don't have any idea what to do in the future. All this happened to us only because of that bloody phone. Actually not even because of it but because of me. I was the one to promise to rob for Mr. Dean, something which I didn't even have any proof for. Wait! What happened to him! I last saw a driver beating the hell out of him and on the other hand, he not even touching him. In hurdle, I called the nurse in a high pitched voice and asked her if she saw any man with brown color attire. "We saw him fighting with someone on the road and the security and hospital officials called the police right on time, before the fight turned into something really big!" she replied. "Where is he right now?" I asked again. "In the police station of course!" she replied. "Listen madam, I need to get going now, I have to leave for the Police Station" I talked nonsense. "Have you lost your mind? You just had an open chest 3 hours ago! We can't allow you to leave before 4 days!" she replied, as she tried to show affection. What should I do now? I have my Mom here, who just suffered a paralysis, my chest suffering with 4 stitches and Mr. Dean waiting for me in the police station. It was Tuesday today and I had to go to the museum tomorrow with the school and steal the Murcaxro. How strange it felt saying this? The hospital officials also won't allow me to leave the hospital, at least before 4 days. What could I do now? I saw a bottle of chloroform on the table. Slowly, I got up from the bed and picked up the bottle. I plucked my handkerchief out from the back pocket of my pants and rinsed it with the chloroform. I myself wore a surgical mask and walked down to the nurse, who was still reading the very 2nd page. I carefully called her and made a short contact of the handkerchief with her nose, which made her sleep 'A Good Dream'. I started to move out of the room and luckily no one was out. I walked bare feet on the cold tiles and finally made it to the downstairs. Fortunately, no one gave me a good notice and I was successful in escaping. I wanted to have a look at Mom but declared that it was good if I returned before 1 or maximum 2 hours as the doctor already informed. I wanted to go in a cab as I had never been to the Police Station before. Therefore, I booked a cab and reached the Police Station in Lane

No. 15. I walked in and asked the officer, "Excuse me sir, is anyone namely Dean Denbrough present here?" The male officer, with 14 inch biceps and full bearded face, took a fierce look at me and said, "So you are his friend, right? No issue. Some of his other two friends came and got him from here." "Sir what about the one he was fighting with?" I inquired. "Oh! I have no idea about him" he replied. "Sir, do you have any idea where they might be off to?" I asked question upon questions. "How the hell on Earth can I know that? Now just get out of my station!" he exclaimed with big red eyes. I was afraid and quickly made my way out of 'his' station. Just as I came out, a man with full leather jacket pulled me inside a small street and this scared me a bit only, because in the past 24 hours, I decided to rob in a guarded museum, sent my Mom into paralysis and escaped from a Hospital for the cost of a nurse [I was afraid if she woke up]. Thus, it was now no big deal for a stranger to pull me or push me, no matter for what reason. The handsome looking man spoke first, "Kazuo Tanaka…Heard a lot about you from Dean! I am Jon Joe and here, my friend Stan Haley!" I started to move back just like I used to when I first met Mr. Dean. "Hey don't be afraid man…I am here." I looked back and saw Mr. Dean standing by. "Mr. Dean, what is all this and who are these guys?" I asked him. "First of all, I am sorry for that brawl which occurred on the road, I really had no idea! Well these are the two friends of mine whom I was talking about!" he replied. "Tomorrow is a very special and life changing day in your life buddy, are you ready for it?" said the guy whose name was Stan. "Why? What is it tomorrow?" I asked him directly with confidence. "It's Wednesday tomorrow and you have to visit the museum... I think you better got the reference" said Jon. "Oh yeah, I remember" I giggled. He then added "But there is something important you need to go through before...a plan!"

6. A ROBBERY FOR GOOD... I GUESS

"Mr. Dean, I really need to talk to you about that. Will Mom allow me to…?" I asked him. "No worries Kazuo. Your Mom is good and she won't really stop you from getting what you should get, what is yours by all rights!" he replied. "Oh really?" I asked as I didn't knew how bad it could go if I wasn't serious. "Lend me your ears so that I can narrate the plan!" said Jon interrupting me in my curiosity. He then added, "The museum has 3 floors including a ground floor, a basement for parking, 10 doors for exit with armed guards, 4 doors for emergency exit and more than 150 CCTVs. We will manage to go anyhow into the building but the rest of the game lies on Kazuo then. The room where the Murcaxro is has a roof made up of wooden tiles, about which no one has any idea. Stan will hack the CCTVs of the room and those of the main entrance so that there is no issue in escaping." He narrated it so simply but was it possible? Then I raised a question, "But what about the sirens and the guards and why did you only choose for the main door except for the Emergency exit ones? They had less chances of having any security…" The way I asked 4 questions in a single breath made me feel proud that I should have a master degree in robbery. Then Stan replied, "After stealing the painting, the security sirens will buzz immediately and most of the security will assume that we will opt for the Emergency exits or secret exits and while they will be focusing on them, we will escape through the main one." For the first time in 15 minutes, Mr. Dean spoke, "Hopefully, it gets easier than you told." he then gave me a look, as if I was the one planning. Then I said for the second time, "Hey Mr. Jon, how will I break the wooden tile of the roof for you to jump out. There will be teachers, students, museum officials and guards around." "You don't need to break the roof when everyone will be around, you need to open it when no one will be around" he replied. Then Stan added, "It is all about probability. All of this needs to be as smooth as possible. One mistake from anyone, and we all rot in the Black Prison for life." This statement shivered me. "Kazuo, are you ready boy?" Mr. Dean asked. "Huh" I replied rudely but he didn't understand. "Ok boy, you need to go normally to the museum tomorrow, walk and talk normally and most important, after handing over the painting to us, you need to go back with your fellows so that no one doubts you" said Jon. "Ok, I think that tomorrow is a big day then. Let's have some rest. Kazuo, Stan will drop you back to the Hospital. I already have paid your Hospital bills" said Mr. Dean. "Thanks a lot Mr. Dean...I can never repay you enough for what you did for us..." I replied emotionally. "Dear, I am your uncle. You never need to lend to your uncle, right?" he replied emotionally as well. "Come on you 'senti-masters' now. Kazuo, come, let me drop you back to the Hospital" said Stan. It felt like this was my family now. My robber's academia. Stan dropped me back to the Hospital and soon I was back in my room. The nurse was still sleeping and I lay on the bed as I never had wakened before. Just after 15 minutes, the doctor came in and said, "So, how are you dear? Oh! Why is this girl sleeping?" "Don't know. She might be tired after all this running," I replied. "Well I need to talk to the management about this behavior of her. Though after a deduction in her salary she might come to senses!" he warned as he took the decision in my pressure. "No need to do that, I am good sir!" I said, trying to be good. After all I was the one behind displacement in her sleeping schedule. "Well how is my mother now?" I asked. "Yes that is what I came here to talk about. She came to her senses and started to shout for you. We again calmed her down with a dose of anesthesia. She will have a peaceful sleep for the night and will wake in around 18-20 hour" said the doctor. "I hope she is fine now?" I asked. "Yeah, there is nothing to worry. You also have some rest now" he suggested. The nurse woke just at the moment and the doctor gave a shameful sight at her. Without talking, she and the doctor left my room, leaving me alone for the night. I stopped thinking about the past as well as the future. As usual, I gave a smile to the blue colored wall and slept. It was the biggest running day of my life tomorrow. I was scared but still excited.

I woke up around 7:00 AM and started to look for...toothbrush. The rude nurse came in and she handed me over a greenish blue color one. She left the room and I entered the washroom. Unlike other hospitals, this was a private one with neat and clean rooms. I took around 30 minutes in the washroom and came out. I had my breakfast in 15 minutes until I got a call at the phone. It was Mr. Dean. "Kazuo, we are waiting for you outside the main gate of the hospital. Make it quick or your schoolmates will leave for the school without you," he said. Honestly, I forgot about it and started to move slowly out of the room. Mr. Dean had already paid my and Mom's hospital bills. All the doctors and nurses had the night shift and thus they were taking a little nap other than some officials and sweepers. It didn't take me much effort in escaping but I wanted to see Mom first. I went straight into her room and it felt like she had a good sleep that night. I crawled downstairs because now I could feel a little pain on my stitches. I had a surgical mask on my face so that no one could think that I was a serious patient who had an open chest 12 hours ago. The more I tried to look good, the more pain I felt in the whole left side of mine. A little struggle and I was able to see Mr. Dean's car with Jon sitting on the driver's seat, Mr. Dean on the front seat and Stan...No! Stan wasn't there. The moment I pushed the door, an official got me by my hand. "Hey little buddy, where are you heading to?" he asked in a friendly tone. "Hey, he's with us. I called him here!"

cried Mr. Dean. "But who are you sir?" he inquired. "I am Dr. Dean. How the hell is it possible that you don't know me? Let me deal with you later. Now spare that kid!" said Mr. Dean, in a little overacting angry mode. "Sorry sir, you can go kiddo" the official commanded the order in hesitation. I came out of the glass door and Mr. Dean smiled at me. "Come on quickly, make it to the back seat" he said. "Mr. Dean, are you really a doctor?" I asked innocently. He and Jon burst out in a big and silly laughter. "That's why I like you boy, you are really nothing more than a naive pigeon" he said. "Ok I am sorry but where is Stan?" I asked. "He has already made it to his special room where he can hack the CCTVs" Jon replied. "Won't he be there with us?" I again questioned. "No buddy. Now tell me the directions of your school!" he commanded. I narrated him at each and every corner until we were standing opposite to the entry gate of my school. "Now go and listen...Don't hesitate!" said Mr. Dean and for the first time, he kissed me on my forehead. I entered inside and the school felt like a new place for me. I walked 22 steps and was about to receive a punch on my face before my reflex could defend it and return the favor with a punch of my own. He surely had to be Steve and yes he was! For the first time, Steve ran away in fear! I made it to the hall where the students were waiting for the bus to arrive so that they can leave for the museum. I held the phone tightly in my pocket. "Kazuo!" a sharp, loud voice echoed through my left ear. From a distance I could see Zhen running to me. It felt like a Road-roller about roll flat a road which in the next 5 seconds would be me. Zhen made it nearer to me and grabbed me in his arms. "Where have you been for all this time? I really missed you man!" he exclaimed. "I too buddy. Hope you are doing well" I replied in a happy tone. "It has been a long time since I saw you!" Zhen said, his emotions bursting out. "Buddy, it has only been some days. Actually I wasn't feeling comfortable coming to school these days..." I corrected myself and informed him which was ultimately going to reveal a very deep secret for him. "Why? Oh! Let me guess, is it because of Steve?" Zhen asked. "No. A few minutes back I just punched the taste out of his mouth!" I replied. "Don't tell me. Was it for real? I should have been there watching all that happen!" he said surprisingly. Being honest, I myself was surprised with my answer. Did I really punch the gangster of our school? No way. "So Kazuo, are you ready to accompany us to the museum today?" Zhen asked. "Yeah, but I forgot to bring everything except for one... " I said. "Ok, so what is it?" "It's my bag man!" I replied. "But how the hell is that possible? Weren't you at home these days?" he asked with a breath of curiosity. I didn't found it a better idea to narrate him everything so I continued to lie. "No actually I had an outing with my far-living uncle. He dropped me at the school very early this morning"

7. WELCOME TO THE GAME

"Ok students. It's time to leave for the place. The seniors will board Bus no.1 and the juniors will board Bus no.2" the teacher said. Zhen had to board Bus no.1, so he won't be with me. I still was afraid, thinking of Steve. Will he avenge me for that insult or will he hide himself from me? Come on! Watching good dreams Kazuo Tanaka! "Zhen and Kazuo, what are you two doing there? Come on, be quick!" one of the teachers screamed. I entered the bus. I didn't saw Steve anywhere but finally my eyes caught him sitting quite calmly on the backseat. He didn't utter a word, though I knew he saw me. It took us one and a half hour to reach the museum. It was all framed with thick metal walls, bulletproof glasses, 25 CCTVs for one sector and 6 sectors in total. The ground floor had all rooms for the officials and management class. The 1st floor stored some important weapons, books and information from different war periods. The 2nd floor had the real red apple, what we were in search of, the Murcaxro. "Ok students, you want to see the other masterpieces first or go straight to the finishing desert?" asked the teacher. "Sir, I think we should go to see the Murcaxro first!" said Zhen. "Everyone sure?" the teacher asked. Everyone agreed to the decision. Therefore, we left for the 2nd floor. The moment I was about to walk, the phone beeped. It was a call from Mr. Dean. "Hello, are you in position Kazuo?" he asked. "We just left for the 2nd floor where the painting is. Will you direct me further?" I replied. "No. On watching you with the phone, you could be suspected. We will let it be as smooth as possible" he stopped and then added, "When you reach the place, you are going to see a hexagonal room..." "Where the painting is actually, right?" I added quickly. "No, where you are going to see two tin plates! One of them has a matchbox beneath it. Use it and burn the plates. It will result in the complete smoking of the room" he corrected me and explained the plan. "But if someone caught me doing it, what would it result in?" I asked. "That's why boy, if I were you, I would make it really quick and of the CCTVs, well...The 2nd floor has really no CCTVs at all!" he replied. "What? Are you kidding me?" I asked with complete surprise. "No, I am not kidding" he said. Then what is Stan going to do there if there are really no CCTVs in there. I was really confused. The painting which costs more than a bungalow has no CCTVs around it for sure safety. Something was absolutely fishy in the voice of Mr. Dean while he was saying this. Anyway, I still carried on with my work.

"Students, here we have reached the 2nd floor where the Murcaxro is. I hope that you'll maintain perfect shape of discipline in here. Will you?" the teacher asked. "Yes sir..!" everyone replied in one voice. It was a big and long corridor with tall walls. I barely could see the end of it and that's why it had more than 20 rooms. Which room I had to go in for those tin plates? I remember Mr. Dean saying that it was a hexagonal room. I don't know if it was my fortune but the rooms didn't have any doors. Therefore it was easy to find out the place. After walking almost 40 steps, a diversion came. All the students were excited, the teachers were in position but I was pretty scared, and why I won't be? I escaped the Hospital after a panic attack, for the first time I didn't heard the voice of Mom since the last 2 days and all of that, I was about to give light to the biggest event of my normal life.

The students went through the right path and I was left alone in the middle of the way. "Hey Kazuo, are you coming or not?" one of my classmates asked. "Just two minutes, let me look at some other pieces first. Well, have you seen Zhen?" I asked. "Yeah, I last saw him going to the rest room" he replied and chased the mob. I asking him about Zhen was only to divert his attention from my body standing idle there. I started walking towards the left path and after one minute and twenty-four seconds I took a look to my right side and found a room painted in white with tall, hexagon shaped walls. I hunched that this was the room which Mr. Dean was talking about. I checked from the open area, if there were any CCTVs hanging around in the walls. No! There weren't any! Was I dreaming? One of the best museums in our state, having nil level of security in one of its most precious room! I could've never imagined that! I slowly entered the room. I tried to look for the plates and I found both of them lying on the floor. How Mr. Dean did knew that there were some plates in here. Anyways, I picked the first one up and found nothing beneath. Then after I picked the second one, I found a red matchbox stick to it with blue colored paper tape. I peeled it off and just the moment, Mr. Dean called. "Hey kiddo, you found it?" he asked immediately. "Yeah, it was really difficult to find this room in the endless corridor" I replied. "Ok, just execute the plan which I narrated you earlier and after you burn the plates, run back to the place where your friends and teachers are" he said. "You mean where the Murcaxro is, right?" I corrected him. "Yeah it can also be said that way, where Zhen is!" he tried to be a little over smart. Wait how Mr. Dean did come to know about Zhen. I don't remember a time when I told Mr. Dean about him. I thought it was better to ask. "Mr. Dean how you…" and he disconnected the call in my mid sentence. Something from my inside told me that what I was about to do was absolutely wrong, but the bucket of my sins had reached to a limit where I can't backup now. I took out three matchsticks from the box, sparked them twice and lit the plates on fire. At first they gave out really negligible amount of smoke but within ten seconds it started to increase at a high rate. I was worried if it could harm something but then I noticed alarms ringing. I looked around to the entrance wall and up from it came out a little and cute…CCTV camera. Was it that Mr. Dean lie to me? No. I refuse to accept that. He had all of his belief in me and I had all of mine in him. I left my mother alone in the Hospital just for him, I came running with a stitched chest just for him and this is what is happening to me now? In fear, I quickly called him. "Hello Kazuo" he said first, "Thanks for helping me out but, it has overturned on you now!"

8. IT HAS OVERTURNED KAZUO..!

"Hello, hello. Mr. Dean, what's all this happening around. The alarms started to rang, a mini CCTV emerged from the top of the ceiling and now..." "Listen Kazuo" he interrupted me, "I am sorry. That's it. I, for the first time, feel really ashamed of my actions, my emotions and all of that my lies. It was my plan to get to you and then to the Murcaxro with your help, that's all I have to say. I am sorry and I love you" he said. For the next three and half seconds, it felt like I was all alone in this world and the Earth was slowly sinking beneath my feet. "What? Have you lost your mind? You can't do this to me now! I want you to take me out now. NOWWW!" I exclaimed but it was useless because he had already disconnected the call. Within 2 minutes I was surrounded by 10 security guards, my schoolmates, my teachers but my eyes couldn't see Zhen around."Get your hands up and don't try to move you little rascal!" one of the security guards said. It was the first time, except for Zhen and Steve that someone had abused me, and this was all because of that bloody Dean. It was a mistake honoring him with the word 'Mister'. "I want to see your damn hands up!" the guard screamed again. I was still in shock on watching the situation I right away was in but still, I slowly managed to up my hands because his voice tone declared that his next step would be a bullet shot right on my stitched chest. "Officers, I think you are dealing with a false situation. He's a boy from our school. May I know his allegation please?" one of my teachers asked. "Just heard the alarms ringing and we rushed down to this room." he replied, with a little down tone. "It's possibly a by chance mistake. Forgive him for this once please!" the teacher requested. It was clear in his eyes that he felt ashamed because of me. "Nobody of you moves! We are seriously going to take down..." BEEP. He never finished his sentence. Again some alarms started to ring. This time the voice came from the left side of the long corridor. Everyone started to run towards the site of alarming. I was left alone with some of my schoolmates, teachers and complete armed guard. After one minute, the Walkie Talkie of a guard sounded with the voice of another guard. "Guard 202, the painting Murcaxro is missing. We have an emergency right now!" "What is the matter officer? We are heading towards the site of theft!" he said on his talkie. "Half of the guards follow me to the room and others stay here with this lad and his mates. Don't let anyone out and call the police immediately!" he said in one complete breath. How the hell on Earth was that possible. I was here, so who stole the Murcaxro. Maybe, it could be a man from the 'Rob Office' of Dean, maybe he just used me as a pawn, but for now, I had to concentrate on myself and the situation I was in. It didn't felt very friendly. It was always that my bus mates, classmates and in fact some of my teachers gave a dirty look to me without any reason but on such a big defame of mine as well as theirs, they didn't gave me any dirty look but something worse than that. It reflected in their eyes that how they felt right away. I didn't put my hands down, though the guns were already. I wanted to show them that I realized my mistake, but it was too late. "Officers, there's the boy, innocent looking but with high guts. TAKE HIM!" said the guard who earlier left for the theft site. Behind him came four police officers but they weren't normal ones. They were all puffed up with air and I remember one of them with the 14 inch bicep whom I met in the Police Station, the day back. "So…You are having a good time in here, trying to rob things! Well, I appreciate your bravery but it has no place for law. Leon, take him!" he said and commanded the other officer. Before my school mates could understand the situation and the police officer could take his handcuffs out to tighten them in my wrists, another Police Officer came in. His tag showed his name as 'Mayaan Denbrough- Inspector, Naperville Police Station'. "Excuse me officers, please allow us to check the CCTV footage first of all. We'll decide the rest factors later" he said. "Are you sure?" the police officer confirmed. "Yes, I'm. No need to take this adolescent" he replied. "Ok, but on your guarantee only sir" he replied like he was about to set me free and a wave of mint breath went through my throat. "Yeah, for sure!" he replied. As the police left, the official took me to the CCTV room. It had more than 20 TVs placed next to each other. "Ok, show me the footage, 20 minutes ago of Room no. 17, 2nd floor" he told the operator. The footage opened right on the scene when I burned the plates and the smoke spread over the place. After watching it, he told me, "Ok, I know you didn't do it deliberately. Either you lost your senses or you did it in force by someone. What was it, tell me?" I was shocked on hearing this. Was he a part-time psychiatrist or else? "Sir, how do you…" I stopped my tongue in the middle. "Well, I think I got a clarification now. Come on, spill, shoot!" he said in a strange voice. It took around 15 minutes for me to narrate him the whole story. He listened very carefully. "Ok, got it. Well, for now your schoolmates and teachers are waiting for you down. Break down that damn phone to pieces and live a normal life again. I let you go for now but the Murcaxro is missing and all the doubts have fall upon you. It's our as well as your responsibility to get it back. Is that clear, my dear?" he said. I was down again and the Earth which was sinking beneath my feet was now in place. "Ok sir, I'll try my level best!" I said, though I didn't knew how to?

9. THE FIRST AND LAST CHANCE.

"Well sir, can I see the footage of the room where the Murcaxro is?" I asked him. "Oh yeah, of course we have forwarded the footage on social media and advertisement display-boards" he replied but struck in middle of the sentence. "Well sir, what's the problem then? You have got each and everything in here to deal with this problem. Why me then?" I asked, tackling his earlier statement. "Hey boy, this is not a problem. For you, it is an opportunity to prove yourself after all this which happened just an hour ago and yes, you could also track those rascals down. The thief might have been their second option other than you" he replied with angry-confidence. Well, if looked at the brighter side, he was right. I could kill two sparrows with one stone only if I find the one who stole the Murcaxro. "Ok sir, I will take your leave now, but what if I need to communicate with you?" I asked him. "Well, are you looking for me to give you some sort of mobile phone?" he said laughingly. "Of course...not, but still, if really urgent, then what to do?" I asked hesitatingly, because I thought he, for sure, would insult me. He stood silent for some seconds and then spoke. "If that's the matter, just come to my place. House no. 15, Blue Ladder Park,

Naperville on your weekends and I hope you'll have your summer holidays going on from day after tomorrow so you can really manage. I'll be waiting" he said. I quickly took a note of the address. From his talks, he looked very nice but we never know the inside of a person. I have already dealt with one such guy, you know. I would try not to name him anymore in my so called 'normal life'. "Thank you sir! It really meant a lot. You took a guarantee for me, listened to my guilt but all of that, you also gave me another chance. It was absolutely unexpected. I owe you a big one" I said, tears falling off my eyes. "It's ok my dear, I saw it in your eyes that you weren't the one behind this whole damn thing. It was just a duty, which I completed" he replied happily. "Excuse me sir, I had actually asked you for one more favor!" I emphasized the earlier request. "Please, let me know!" he replied quickly. "Can I please see the CCTV footage of that thief? I only mean it so that I could get some hint," I requested. "Oh yeah, I'm sorry, just forgot!" he replied. He started the clip and for the first 10 seconds, nothing happened, but after that. A guy, dressed fully in black, showed up. It really didn't felt that he was dressed black but painted in the color. I meant that every part of his was tightly packed in the black and blue stripped costume other than his hands. Then I noticed a thing. The man had seven fingers in his left hand, with which he held the painting. Then, could it be him? Thousands of thoughts hit my brain, right on the cerebrum. Within, 20-30 seconds, I time-travelled my traumatic past and was now imagining the traumatic future. The only guy I had seen in the very world with seven fingers was only, Zhen.

"Hey little buddy, are you fine? Looks like you have turned pale!" Mayaan uncle asked in a tense voice. "Ye...Yeah, I'm fine! I just noticed a thing but I need to research on it first" I said openly. "I hope it'll not affect you that severely" he exclaimed passionately. "No problem at all. Ok, thank you sir. I take your leave now" I said, still not in my conscious. "Ok dear, take care and remember to come to my place. You are always welcome there" he replied back in a happy tone again. "Thanks for everything. Goodbye" I said and ended the conversation. As I was walking towards my bus, I was going back to the nostalgias of me and Zhen, from enjoying breaking glasses while playing baseball to poking Steve every time. I was neutral at this point but I need to look in this matter first, because I wouldn't judge very soon. "Hey Kazuo, come fast. We were about to fetch for you! Are you ok?" a boy said, who was coming for me after all the time I spent in the CCTV room. "Yeah buddy, I am coming. Thanks for your concern!" I replied, still lost in other thoughts. I started to follow him until both of reached the parking where our bus was waiting. I entered the bus and tried to make no eye contact with anyone and leaned myself towards the Seat no. 1. To my surprise, everyone started to come near me and pat my shoulder to encouragement. I was super surprised but still, I held no expressions. Finally, I saw Steve coming nearer and nearer. I thought he was about to return the favor of the punch I landed on his nose the morning, but no... Steve grabbed me by the collar of my shirt and hugged me. Everyone started applauding. Was that they had already discussed how to deal with me the moment I enter the bus? "I believe in you my friend. We, though sometimes might act bizarre with you but we trust you. Only we have got the right to beat you, not any bloody stranger!" he said and fake-laughed, tear drops hanging from his eyes. "I am sorry, for everything!" he murmured in my ears. Both of us broke to tears. It felt like I had some backup already built. In no time, the applauding turned into hooting and for the first time in years, I smiled in the school bus. The bus left the museum in around 10 minutes and I sat comfortably with my friends whom I earlier called my classmates. I found it better not to narrate them the whole tale, so I controlled my temptation. Within 1 hour, we reached the school and it was me who touched the land first. The moment we arrived, our Principal came near me and was about to slap me hard but the teachers who also arrived along, cried from a distance not to. They narrated him the story. He then again came near me but I started to step back. "It's ok son. I just heard the first half of the story, I am sorry" he said. I smiled a bit. I thereafter walked to the teacher of the senior classes. "Sir, can you please tell me where is Zhen?" I asked him. "Oh, the huge friend of yours! Well his uncle had come to receive him outside the museum door, so we let him go." he replied. What the hell! I know Zhen since the last 7 years and as far as my information holds, he only owes a pet dog Rogers to be called any near one other than me. How did this uncle of his emerge from then? Things have started to get confusing now. How many small, breath-taking, confusing and concept turning stories are actually in this large one, which I call my life? Well for now, I think I need to get going to the Hospital. Mom might be missing me.

10. GOING BACK WHERE IT STARTED..!

I thought of running to the Hospital but it was 7 kilometers away. I couldn't afford that with my stitches. I checked the left pocket, nothing there. Then I checked in the right pocket and found a bunch of wrinkled 50$. I came out of the main gate of the school and crossed the road to the opposite side. After 5 minutes, a taxi arrived and I started to bargain the amount just like Mom used to. He finally agreed on 40$ and I comfortably got in the cab. I wasn't in a mood to talk but still, to flourish it, I originated the conversation. After 30 minutes, I could see the front gate of the Hospital. As soon as the cab stopped, I jumped out of it, made the payment, received the rest of the money and ran towards the Hospital. A guard stopped me on my way and started to ask irrelevant questions. I answered whatever came on tongue and ran again. Everyone was watching me, running with a speed of 20 km/hr. It made them felt like some relative of mine was critically injured or he/she had passed away but the reason was something else. I could never have imagined that I will kick my responsibilities just for that freak... Nobody stopped me except for the nurse who used to attend me. "Hey boy, where were you? Have you gone nuts? With a stitched chest and running here and there!" she exclaimed. Maybe, she had no idea that I had left the Hospital this morning. I think she thought that I was having a walk. "Oh I am sorry! I was just feeling vexed lying on the bed all day" I replied with confidence. "It's ok. Just go and have some rest again" she replied and I got my hunch confirmed. I think that her irresponsible behavior had benefited me this time. I walked to my Mom's room and slid the door a bit. I found nothing except for the fragrance of her favorite perfume. I checked in washroom. It was clean and unused because the floor wasn't wet but dry. I asked one of the compounder about her. "Oh, that lady! She was really funny and we miss her" he replied. A cold vibration went down my spine. "What do you mean?" I asked in frustration. "Hey man, I mean she was departed an hour ago. It was a normal paralysis and she herself insisted to let her go, only on her assurance" he added quickly. My muscles got relaxed. If Mom was departed, then for sure she would have gone home. I thought of leaving as well but my departure was on the day after tomorrow. It could be that now these lads could doubt me if I disappeared and also, I felt little pain again on the right side of my ribs. I somehow managed to walk to my earlier room. A nurse was sitting on my bed with a magazine in her hand. I stood in front of her and for the next 10 seconds, she neither talked nor got up from the bed. "Excuse me lady, will you please let the patient lie on the bed. I have 4, maybe more stitches on my chest!" I informed which indirectly embarrassed her. "Yes please, I'm sorry" she said. I sat on the bed and slowly pushed myself to the pillow. I told the nurse to give me my evening medicine schedule. I think she was a little more awake and responsible than the earlier one. She got me three tablets and one syrup bottle. I got them down my throat and slept.

As for the next day, I just kept looking at the wall clock. From 10 AM to 9 PM. It wasn't an exhausting day at all but yet boring one.

It was finally time for me to say goodbye to all the ill smell around the Hospital. I ran down to the reception area. They checked my due. It was zero. Thank God that piece of idiot hadn't deceived me here. He already had paid the bills and completed the formalities. I came rushing out of the Hospital but there were only 10$ in my pocket. I actually wanted to walk because from the last two days, I was either sleeping or playing with my fingers all the time in my bed. So, I found it better, thinking it would improve my health. Within 1 hour and 30 minutes, I reached my old, smelly lane. I now realized the importance of them. My legs started to tremble but I couldn't hold them. Mom literary just used to beat me if I was 15 minutes late. In this case, I was exactly 3 days, 9 hours and 30 minutes late. It would be better if I suicide than what Mom was going to do to me. I walked up the steel stairs and with all my effort, knocked the door. No reply for the next 1 minute. I knocked again.

No reply again. A sense of fear than knocked me! I pushed open the door and went straight to the living room, then towards the kitchen. I saw Mom sitting on the rocking chair, with a pair of ear buds in her ears. I cried her from the back, "Mom!" She saw me and came running, grabbed me in her arms, kissed my forehead but didn't wept.

As a son, who was out of her sight from last 3 and half days, I was expecting that she would cry but she didn't. "Where were you Kazuo?" she asked in anger and slapped me hard. I gobbled an air of satisfaction. "I am sorry Mom; it'll take me time to narrate what actually happened!" I replied. After an hour of here and there talking and the narration of the story, she asked me. "I don't care what we are facing or what we are going to end up like but, will you start robbing things then? I brought you up without your Dad and this is what you want to do thereafter?" she completed the speech. I really felt ashamed. I wanted to talk but, with what tongue? So I thought it was better for me to remain silent. "Answer me Kazuo!" she cried. "No Mom, I didn't do this deliberately. That brown-wearer piece of crap, who actually is the real culprit of this story and who got us to the hospital when you had the paralysis attack, Dean, he pushed me up to the limits" I replied. "And now, how are you going to find the painting?" she asked "Even I don't know, but yes, I definitely will!" I replied back because now I was a master in agreeing to things I didn't know how to execute. I really didn't expect but after 3 or more hours, things turned out normal. She talked and acted normally. Mom had really changed a lot. Later, when she was mopping the floor with a pair of ear-buds in her ears, I finally took the risky step and asked her, "Mom, are you ok?" She took one of the buds out and asked back, "I beg your pardon, I wasn't listening". Yes it was for real that she had no excitement or surprise for all of this which happened to us. "I am asking that 'Are you ok?'" I again asked. "Yeah I am good. Everything alright, why are you asking me?" she replied. "No, actually, I thought that you seem to be a bit changed!" I said. "Really? I didn't expect you saying this" she replied. "No I mean from the inside. You look hard-hearted now" I said under the pressure of my heart. "What rubbish…" she said but then, there was an awkward silence for some seconds. Something was there which pricked her from the inside. "Mom, tell me" I requested. "What Kazuo?" she asked back hesitatingly. "The feeling, which you are trying to hide" I asked back a bit philosophically. "There's nothing you idiot!" she declared with confidence. I looked at her with the same stare which I every time used to spill a secret out of her. This stare was my hidden weapon and it every time helped me out. Any time if I used this, within few seconds, she would burst into laughter. I used it sometimes when she came back from the shop to confirm that she hadn't bought anything which was against our budget. But when I observed, she wasn't laughing, not even smiling. I saw that Mom looked tensed. I couldn't bear, so I again asked with sympathy, "Mom, tell me, what is it?" I asked. "Kazuo, I am afraid. What is all this going? A man enters our life, asks you to rob him a painting, giving the name of your father, then deceive you and in the end, you doubt on your best friend Zhen to steal it! Can it be that all of this is inter-related?" she replied back logically. Of course, Mom had a point! Can this all be inter-related? There was a 99% chance of saying 'yes' to it! "Mom, let me think about this. Though you might be right!" I replied with a good level of confidence.

11. BACK TO NORMAL...

For the rest of the day, I was sitting on my study table, drawing tree-graphs, charts, thread-pins and many innovative techniques. If crime investigators would take a look at my room, they would doubt me for a serial killer. I mentioned everything, the chances of people having seven fingers; how Dean did know my father and his business and many more questions like that. Luckily, our summer vacations are going to start from tomorrow and l will get plenty of time to work on this.

I continued on the details until I realized that it was sharp 1:00 AM, but I didn't felt sleepy. Still, I thought that I should have some rest. I lay straight on the bed and for the next 10 minutes, stared my side table. Will Mom come tomorrow with the coffee mug and newspaper, with a 'job offer' inside like routinely? Sudden thoughts changed my mind and lifestyle but I didn't want Mom to change. I lost my Dad, my relief, my belief in people but not my hope. I know if I lose it, then I lose everything. Now I had friends, a support to not let me fall which made me proud of myself. As usual, I looked at the wall, smiled and slept.

Some beams of the sunlight fell on the window of my room and slowly started to bend towards the floor. Two sparrows were sitting on the electric wire, only chirping. I stared the roof, thinking nothing until I heard a knock on my door. My lips automatically lifted up to a smile as I saw Mom enter, the coffee mug in her right hand and the newspaper in her left. She started talking about job offers as usual and it didn't seem like she was worried about me or anything else. I didn't hear a single thing, only smiled and bowed at the completion of her every sentence. Then she stopped and said, "Be careful, the coffee is hot! Also, get ready and have a walk. Though you might feel fresh after all this, by inhaling some fresh air..." A sense of relief and freshness drove through my body. She was same and will remain same.

After I was done with my bath, I sat on the couch for breakfast. Mom got me some toasts along with a small mug of Hot Chocolate. I enjoyed the great feast and then switched on the TV. I changed channels, one after another until I finally stopped on a 'local-news channel'. I sat relaxed on the couch unlike my heart. Just the moment, Mom showed in and unplugged the TV. "I think you didn't hear clearly what I told you to do? Just go out and have some fresh morning air. You can't waste your summer vacations, only sitting on the couch all day and doing nothing!" she said in one, single breath. "No, I already heard you saying that, just forgot. I am sorry!" I replied with ease. "Ok, then go now...Maybe, you'll find some mates out as well" she replied back. I took out my brand new sneakers from my cupboard. I always wondered that how did

Mom managed to get me all the delicacies in the world even with such small salary? I took a look towards her innocent face. She was too beautiful to work. Finding a part-time job and working was for losers like me! "Mom…" I called her from a distance. "Huh?" she replied back with a sigh. "I am ready to work on a part-time job. Wherever and whenever you tell" I added quickly to the silence. "What? You are kidding, aren't you?" she asked with surprise. "Yeah, we deserve better and I can go to any limit for that…" I said. She didn't say anything. Just smiled and then hugged me. We were one and we belonged together.

I wore my sneakers and jogged down the stairs. I started with a simple, brisk walk and then stopped somewhere. I took a look to my right. The lane was still there. It was the same lane where I met him for the first time. Everything was there, the Bio-degradable dustbin, the smell and the tall walls of two buildings except for him only. I took a deep breath and started to walk again. Now I didn't encouraged myself to live in the past as it only stored his lies. I have to move forward. As I started to walk, I found two of my friends. I continued to walk and soon, they saw me. "Hey Kaz, what's going on! Where are you going?" one of them asked. It was for the first time that I heard someone else other than Mom and Dad to shorten my name, but I loved it. I had no friends first and I also didn't know how they felt for me. But now, things were starting to change. All of my so called classmates were now my friends. They called me names, not to tease me but to make me happy. They didn't give me any dirty looks anymore rather; they just smiled looking at me. Thank God that museum incident had somehow benefited me. "Oh, hey guys! I was just roaming around, tasting some fresh air. You know it has been a lot, right?" I said and both of them giggled. "So, you want to come with us? We were planning to go to the nearby park today" the other guy said. It has been years since I last went to the park nearby and I really wanted to go. So, I agreed. We talked the whole way towards the park and laughed at silly jokes until we weren't aware that the park gate was by our side. The first day of the vacations was a gift for the children. They loved each other's company and enjoyed to the fullest. Riding on swings, sliding on colorful slides, playing hide & seek and many more games. It felt to me like my childhood was back. I didn't need any 'Robber's group' to be on the top of financial relief. In fact, I realized that money is not everything. What your opinion says, how you see at the brighter side of the dark world is what actually counts in! I was back and better than ever!

All three of us raced into the park, lost in the 'Kingdom of Innocence'. I did all the childish actions, in fact more badly than the infants themselves. It was expected from me as all the passion and wanting to live life to the fullest from all over the years came blazing out. I covered myself in dust, played every known game in the world with my new group of friends, which was growing like a bonfire. I was so deeply thrown into playing that I forgot to have lunch and so did the other children. As the Sun started to set, I realized nothing other than one thing…'I am the best version of Kazuo Tanaka, and that's damn true…'

12. MY MOM...THE BEST ADVISOR

I returned home late. Mom, as usual, was watching TV. I went straight into my room. She was so deeply thrown into her show that she didn't even notice me opening the door and walking in. I decided to take a bath because all the dust in the world was right now residing in my hair. Before that, I crawled back into the living room and tried to fun-mess with her. "BOOM!" I cried loud in her ear. She had no expression except for a savage one. "So you really think I have gone nuts and I didn't saw you enter, right?" she asked in a tone. "Well, to be honest, yeah!" I said and ran to the kitchen, laughing. "Hey Kazuo, you want something to eat or you already had something from outside?" she asked, watching me enter the kitchen. "Yes Mom, I am really losing it with hunger. Can you please get me something to eat? Meanwhile, I will also take a bath" I replied. "Oh sure, it seems looking in your eyes that you have enjoyed really hard today!" she said, taunting me. I didn't reply but gave a huge grin and went to the bathroom.

I got some bad mist out of me after the bath and was about fall asleep if not given food within 10 minutes. Just then, Mom entered with a big tray of meal. Sausages, buns, chicken gravy and a drink. The best colossal I was ever going to have. I ate like a starving Cyclops, then gave Mom a goodnight kiss and went straight to bed. For the first time after a week, I was about to fall in the 'Land of Peaceful Sleep' but then, something struck me. It was Saturday today. I had to meet Mayaan uncle. I took the sticky note out from the pocket of my pants I was still wearing. I hadn't changed them since Thursday. I read it loud as if my mind was dead. Street no. 5, House no. 15, Naperville. I decided to crawl to Mom's room which was next door to mine. She was sitting on the bed, leg on leg and scrolling on her phone. Every time I saw a phone, I don't know why but I had goose bumps emerging. I knocked on the door and then called her, "Mom, may I come in?" "Oh, it's 11:30 right now. Why are you awake?" she asked, keeping the phone on the side table. I entered the room and sat right in front of her. "Well I have already narrated the story to you and each and every incident in it, but I am damn sure that you aren't aware what that museum guy had told me to do on weekends. I am…" I said with a filthy expression before she interrupted me. "He had told you to come to his place in Naperville, right?" Mom replied with a savage smile on her beautiful face. "Huh! But it's gone now so should I go there tomorrow?" I asked for her advice as I already knew what a little help from her wisdom was capable to do. "I don't think so but if you have any contact number available, then we can see" she said. "I am sorry but I have no such availability. I think I should go tomorrow. Can you please borrow me some money then?" I replied, forgetting my 'self proclaimed wise words' for her. "Oh I see! There, reach out to the first pocket of my bag and get 50$ from it" she said with no sign of hesitation. I followed the instructions and took the money. "By the way Mom, why are you giving me 50$. I am not booking a cab so it might take less than that" I said. "Yes, even I know that but insurance is must!" she replied and both of us laughed just like we used to. "And Mom, let me know if there are any part-time jobs available. I already told you, 'I am ready'" I said, breaking the laughter. "Of course darling! You know how good I am at that, right?" she replied and we again laughed. Then I kissed Mom for the second time that night and went straight to my bed, keeping the money on my side table. As a matter of habit, I smiled at them and slept. I knew I was going to have a peaceful night though.

My eye lashes spread upwards and I could see the bright beams of the Sun, trying hard to enter my room. I remained still in the said position and finally kicked the blanket, then slowly crawled to the window curtains and slid them. I roughly counted and found more than twenty sparrows sitting on the same electric wire singing some tunes in opera. I don't know why but I had tears in my eyes. I smiled brighter than the Sun itself and then push opened the window. I breathed the fresh and glossy oxygen until

I was satisfied. After 5 minutes, Mom knocked the door. "Now, if you are satisfied, am I allowed to enter?" she said, giggling. "Literary, I am none to grant you permission, cause you are the 'Eater of Worlds'" I replied back, making a steady statement. "Huh, so you want to have a look at job offers today, don't you?" she asked. "I am not an adult yet! I still have my studies pending!" I replied laughing, trying to be over smart. "You bloody..! Ok, enough kidding now. Here is the newspaper. Check the offers at the bottom on the 4th page after you'll get fresh. Is that ok?" she said. "Ok" I replied in short and cleared the conversation. I went straight into the rest room. After I was done with my 30 minute of meditative rest there as well, I caught the newspaper and made it to the 4th page quickly. My eyes spread like a batter of pancake as I read the offers. 1. Lady Salon part-time from 4:00 PM – 6:00 PM daily. Salary: 1500$ per month. 2. Need Public Washroom cleaner on permanent basis. Salary: 700$ per month. 3. Lion den cleaner at the Burdsbend Private Zoo from 5:00 PM – 7:00 PM respectively. Salary: 1150$ per month. Reading this made me mad, especially the last one. I tore the 4th page, formed a ball of it and kicked it out of the window. All that sparrow-opera playing in my mind vanished once and for all. I made my way to the main hall, red-eyed. Mom was watching TV. "Yes I told you that I do accept to work but at least you should get me some good ones. What are these? I am a student and you expect me to clean Public Washrooms and Lion dens?" I said, out of my senses. "Oh actually, you know...Yes. I expected you to do" she said hesitatingly. "You are surreal! I CAN'T BELIEVE THIS! So you used to introduce such offers to me daily, right? It's a good thing that I never saw them!" I replied in frustration. "Ok, get a job only if you find it worthy for you. Happy now?" she asked, still not angry with my tone of talking. "Huh...Well, I am sorry Mom. You know that I just got vexed reading those job-lists and I threw it all out on you" I said, ashamed of the language I earlier held before her. "It's ok sweetie. You know I love you" she replied. Then she kissed me on the cheek and left the hall, towards the kitchen to get breakfast for me. I checked the time. It was 8:30 AM already. The last train for Naperville used to leave the station at 9:30 AM. I took out all the data I made during this time span. Charts, reports, and information about the phone, everything lay bare in front of me! Though I wasn't able to attain a lot about the phone, I still tried to give my best. It was clear that damn thing was a complete enigma. I had smashed it up to pieces already and threw it in a sewer nearby. It was giving me severe nighmares. I buckled all of it in a small, blue colored kit-bag and went straight to the dining table. I had my breakfast, then hugged Mom and left for the station.

13. MEETING IN NAPERVILLE...

I raced downstairs. The station was 5 kilometres away from our apartment. I checked the time on my wrist watch. 9:00 AM already. It was damn impossible for me to run the 5 kilometre distance in just 30 minutes. I wanted to book a cab but I wasn't sure if I would have enough money left then. I started jogging with a small kit bag hung from my right shoulder. I found it a bit easy at first but then I realized that I was about to fall. My stitched chest started to pain. I haven't told anything about these to Mom since the very beginning. Fortunately a car came and stopped by my side. The driver came running down from the car and caught me by my waist. "Hey bro, are you ok?" he asked. "Pretty much" I replied. "Can I drop you anywhere?" he again asked with sympathy. "Sure, thank you!" I replied, still huffing. He dropped me at the station and left. I again checked the time. It was 9:15 AM. I quickly ran the stairs and made my way to the ticket counter. Last train for Naperville was ready to leave at sharp 9:35 AM, approximately 5 minutes later than the usual one. I bought the ticket for 7$ and waited for the train to arrive. I sat down on a bench. It still felt that my heart was restless. I bought a bottle of flavoured energy-drink and soothed my soul. My stitches were removed but the flesh around it was still loose and delicate. I had a slight reflex of panic attack, which was an easy matter to solve though. The doctors pumped some bottle of sublimated medicine in and my heart got released from the suffocation but still, it was paining because the stitches were recently removed. I waited for the next 10 minutes but the train didn't arrive. Another 5 minutes passed peacefully and nothing came, except for the fresh morning breeze. I kept on waiting and finally, at exact 9:52 AM, the train arrived and I quickly made my way into it. I sat at the window seat and tried to sleep. I wasn't facing any sort of insomnia but I had nothing to do. At first I decided to take a look at the data and information but then I thought of having some rest as I was already thrown a lot deep into it since some days. I rested my head on the window panel and the gentle air tried to carry my hair along. I was thinking of everything, me and Zhen playing marbles in every street of the town. How we became friends. How we parted, though I didn't have any tough confirmation yet. I even remember our last moments with Dad and how his business collapsed. Deep down, I had a worthless heart now, which had rotten, carrying every burden in the world. I wanted to cry but I can't, not because I was brave-hearted but two ladies were sitting right in front of me.

The journey to Naperville felt endless, the lush greenery unwinding like a ribbon through the countryside. My mind buzzed with anticipation and uncertainty. Would Mayaan Uncle truly have the answers I sought? Could he clear my name and salvage my dignity from the tarnish left by the museum incident? Could he really help me or he just invited me for fun?

Finally, as dusk painted the sky in strokes of orange and violet, I arrived in Naperville. The tranquil suburb welcomed me with its serenity, the address on the worn paper guiding me to a charming house nestled amidst tall, swaying trees. My heart raced with a mix of apprehension and eagerness as I approached the door, my hand trembling slightly as I rapped my knuckles against the wood.

"Oh, look what we have here, my lad! You've made it!" Mayaan Uncle greeted me with a warm smile, his eyes twinkling with familiarity.

I never expected him exaggerating my presence along with 'My Lad' as a compliment. Though he looked old but his memory power was unchallengeable for his age group.

"Thank you for inviting me, Mayaan Uncle," I replied gratefully, stepping into the cozy haven that was his home.

The interior felt like a sanctum of knowledge, filled with books, artifacts, and scientific curiosities that whispered tales of exploration and discovery. Mayaan Uncle ushered me to a snug sitting area, and as I settled into the chair, a sense of calm enveloped me. "I am sorry sir...I forgot that I had to visit you yesterday. Actually I was busy gathering the data" I said in a sober voice. "Oh, it's ok... It wasn't necessary to come here on weekends only. You can come anytime!" he replied with his eyebrows smiling. "Thanks! So uncle, if you don't mind me asking, where is your family?" I asked, not able to control my temptation. "Don't know! Maybe my Mrs. might be walking in heavens right now and a son..." he stopped and laughed with a look of loss on his face. "I am so sorry sir! I didn't know" I replied, feeling the same for him. "Oh it's ok. Let's talk now, Kazuo. Tell me everything!" Mayaan Uncle encouraged, his tone gentle and inviting. I recounted the turbulent events of the museum incident, the about-to-occur accusations that had cast shadows over my integrity and the doubts that gnawed at my soul. When I was narrating him, I felt myself, somehow, being drawn back from my own words. What if I really had stolen the Murcaxro? Would I still have been able to justify myself? I was really lucky I hadn't done something extra other than lighting those tin plates! Mayaan Uncle listened attentively, his eyes fixed on me, radiating empathy and understanding. With every word, a weight lifted off my chest, the knots of uncertainty slowly unraveling.

As I finished recounting my ordeal, Mayaan Uncle leaned back in his chair, a contemplative expression on his face. "Ah, the museum incident! I still get a sudden shiver when I think that the Murcaxro is nowhere to be found now!" he began, his voice carrying a reassuring tone, "But fear not, my dear boy. I believe I have something that might cast light on the situation. Those rascals will get tracked down!" he disappeared momentarily, returning with a thick folder cradled in his hands. "This contains data and evidence I've gathered!" he said, passing it to me. "Take your time, go through it. I believe it will restore your faith in your innocence." "Yes uncle, even I have got some data with me. You know that thief, who stole the Murcaxro…He had seven fingers in his left hand. I am ashamed to say but my friend, namely Zhen, also has seven fingers in the same hand and he is the one who gave me the phone. After the robbery, everyone told me that some of his uncle had come to receive him at the museum gate and I have never seen him since. Well I won't accuse him but this can't be a coincidence" I added to his sentence. Suddenly, I noticed his hand shaking and his face turning pale white. "Are you ok sir?" I asked, afraid that he might get a Cardiac Arrest. "Huh...Oh yeah…I, am good," he replied with a fake smile. I smelled it. Something was fishy! With trembling fingers, I leafed through the contents of the folder. Documents, photographs, meticulous notes - Mayaan Uncle's laborious investigation was laid bare before me. Each piece of evidence meticulously compiled, painted a vivid picture, gradually erasing the doubts that had plagued my thoughts for so long. "This is…

incredible!" I breathed, a mixture of astonishment and gratitude swirling within me."I'm glad it helps, son!" Mayaan Uncle said warmly, his eyes crinkling at the corners with a smile but his face still pale. "Remember, the truth always finds a way to emerge."

We spent the hours that followed engrossed in discussion, dissecting the evidence and unraveling the intricate web surrounding the museum incident. Mayaan Uncle's wisdom and guidance provided clarity, dispelling the fog of uncertainty that had clouded my judgment. As the night deepened, I felt a newfound sense of hope blooming within me. With Mayaan Uncle's unwavering support and the concrete evidence he had presented, I could see a path to reclaiming my reputation and comfort my heart, also track the robbers. Before bidding him goodbye, I expressed my heartfelt gratitude to Mayaan Uncle for his unwavering belief in my innocence and the invaluable assistance he had provided. The pale look still hadn't gone anywhere. I thought I should ask him again about his health but the more I asked him, I more of his colors changed. I found it better to leave him alone.

Stepping out into the cool night air, the stars glittering like diamonds in the sky, I felt rejuvenated. Mayaan Uncle's guidance had instilled in me a renewed vigor and confidence. I walked back to the station, comfortably, which was luckily near from his home, as the next train would arrive at exact 9:00 PM.

I bought myself a Hot-Dog and a train ticket obviously. Within 10 minutes the train arrived and I was home accompanied by a sense of closure, a belief in the justice that awaited me.

14. FARTHER I GO, THE NEARER I COME

I walked home, proud and symbolic. The frustration which left my brain thinking 'what if?' was now gone and vanished. I put my foot in my homeland at exact 2:30 AM. I was accompanied with seven more people, all men, who were either overtiming at office or only roaming from one station to another after alcohol consumption. Therefore I didn't found myself secure and tried to sprint out of the station. I had told Mom that I might reach home late but this was unexpected. I had been to Naperville thrice in my childhood and now I came to know why we always left home early, because the 70 km distance was pretty far and unfortunately today, the train was slow. It was impossible that a cab might arrive. I still had 39$ in my pocket but the cabs these days didn't accepted less than 45$. Even when I had to come from my school to the Hospital on Wednesday, the day when the incident took place, the cab driver didn't agree on 35$ at all, thereafter I settled it all down on 40$. I decide to walk the 5 kilometer distance and felt sorry that I should've got a jacket along. I had changed my clothes after a week this morning. Still the woolen sweater didn't make me feel so cold and lonely. Three cars stopped by me and invited me for a lift; I didn't agree. I didn't want myself to be kidnapped, though they were nice by ethics. As expected, my chest started to pain. I fell down on my knees and the kit-bag, which held all those data, evidences and information fell on the road as well. I sat down on the road and no car or bike came by as I dearly wanted a lift now; It didn't matter who it was! Still nothing came. I somehow lifted myself up and started to walk slowly, holding my sweater tightly against my chest. I walked and walked until I checked the time. It showed 3:14 AM and I was about to reach home. 10 more minutes of hard work and I was standing at the footsteps of our apartment stairs. I walked slowly up the stairs so that nobody thinks that I am a thief. I didn't knock, but our door used to get closed and locked up after 9:00 PM. I tried to push it hard and was about to fall flat on the door-mat. The door was open and Mom was standing there, waiting for me, I guess. "Where have you been stupid? Do you have any idea what time it is?" she asked with some love-anger emotions. I checked the time on the wall clock and it showed 3:30 AM in the morning. I didn't know if I would get a chance to sleep or not? "Sorry Mom, the train arrived late and was slow as well. I reached Naperville around 4 O' clock and left at 9:00 PM. I had to walk a distance also, so it took me time," I said, "Have you not slept?" She looked weak by face. I am sure she hadn't had her dinner. I persuaded her to have just a few morsels along with me and after we were done, we left for our respective rooms. I slammed my body on the bed and left it unconscious there.

Sunlight filtered through the curtains, painting my room in soft hues as I reluctantly surfaced from slumber. I glanced at the clock, the digits glaring back at me—12:12 PM. The night had been eventful, returning home near 4 AM after meeting Mayaan Uncle in Naperville, clutching data that held the key to unraveling the theft of the Murcaxro.

The aroma of freshly cooked breakfast wafted through the apartment, and I made my way to the kitchen to find Mom setting the table. She greeted me with a warm smile and a plate piled high with pancakes, the golden syrup gleaming under the morning light. "Late enough to beat the Devil, huh? Well it was expected!" she remarked, concern etched in her voice. "Yeah, just some stuff to take care of, you know!" I replied, my mind still lingering on the encrypted data and the cryptic directions Mayaan Uncle had left me with. I wolfed down breakfast, the pancakes a distraction from the weight of responsibility resting on my shoulders. Deciding to clear my head, I excused myself, promising Mom I'd be back soon.

Stepping outside, the crisp air greeted me and I embarked on a stroll around the neighbourhood. My thoughts raced, trying to make sense of the tangled web of clues and suspicions that surrounded the theft. I continued walking for another 20 minutes. That is when I spotted Zhen's distinctive figure in the distance. It felt like my eyes had seen an oasis in the desert. My throat dried out of saliva and I gained 4 degree in my body temperature. Still, I managed to call him.

"Zhen!" I called out, quickening my pace to catch up with my elusive friend. He turned around, surprise flashing across his face before quickly masking it with a forced smile. "Kazuo! Long time no see! What brings you here?" he asked with that fake smile growing wider on his face. "Hey, you disappeared from the museum that day. What happened?" I pressed my curiosity, getting the better of me. Zhen hesitated, avoiding my gaze. "Oh, uh, my uncle came to pick me up. Family emergency, you know?" he said.

"Oh really? You are better aware than me how good I know you and your background. You have only a pet dog for the name of a family, which I've never heard since our relation as friends," I replied, tackling his statement.

Something didn't add up. His sudden departure after the theft struck a chord of suspicion within me since that day. I was trying my level best to take my anger out slowly and slowly, not caring what a big slap from his even bigger hand could do to me.

"Zhen, I know something's not right. Tell me the truth," I urged, a sense of urgency creeping into my voice. Before he could respond, he attempted to dart away, but I pursued him, my instincts screaming that there was more to this than met the eye. We reached a secluded corner, where Zhen finally relented.

"Okay, Kazuo. But you have to promise not to freak out!" he pleaded, glancing around nervously. "I promise," I assured him, my heart pounding in anticipation of what he was about to reveal.

Zhen took a deep breath. "My only uncle... he's Dean Denbrough." The name hit me like a thunderbolt. Mr. Dean—the man who'd initially approached me, coercing me to steal the Murcaxro. The realization sent a shiver down my spine.

"What the hell!" I cried and two girls walking down the way jumped in surprise. "How you know him? Was that you who stole the painting then?" I questioned, trying to make sense of the connection, still in shock.

"Yes, he's my uncle. I don't have only Rogers to be named as a family. Dean Denbrough, my true blood uncle, he's there as well. I am sorry Kazuo, I did it. Only what my uncle wanted me to do but believe me, I don't know why?" Zhen confessed the guilt and fear evident in his voice. My legs froze. My stitched chest just about to open and let my heart jump out. My hand rose up. SLAP. It did hit hard and for the first time in 7 years, Zhen received something hurtful, that too from me.

"Go and play your freaking game with someone else" I cried and slapped again. His eyes were filled with tears, about to fall anytime. Both of us remained silent for the next 5 minutes until he said first. "I am sorry Kazuo! I am sorry!" and wept his face against my shoulder. He hugged me and I don't know why, but I hugged him too. Whatever he did or whatever he had become, he was still my friend. Both of us wept and the people passing by talked about it. Though I observed, I still couldn't stop. I was storing my tears since long and I got the chance to spill them out today.

Our conversation was abruptly interrupted by the sound of footsteps approaching from behind. I turned to see Mr. Dean, his imposing figure casting a shadow over us.

"Well, well, what do we have here?" Mr. Dean sneered, his eyes flickering with malice. I stood my ground, my mind racing for a way out of this precarious situation. "Mr. Dean, you can't get away with this!" I said bravely.

"Ah, Kazuo, you're as stubborn as they come. Pity you had to meddle in things that didn't concern you," he remarked, his tone icy. As he moved closer, Zhen stepped protectively in front of me. "Leave him alone uncle! I won't let you hurt him!" A tense silence enveloped us, the gravity of the situation sinking in. Mr. Dean got a gun from his back pocket and pointed it towards me. I knew I had to act fast before things spiraled out of control.

15. WHY ONLY I LOST EVERYTHING?

"Shut the hell up Zhen and get back here! I need to shoot this dog!" he said and ended with a monstrous laughter. Zhen touched my hand secretly and ran. I followed him as well. That touch was a sign to run. We ran through the streets where we used to play and the mobs of people, enjoying roadside clown acts. I looked back. Mr. Dean was chasing us but luckily he was a bit far. We ran as fast as we could. Finally, we by-passed my apartment and stopped after some minutes, hiding besides a Bio-degradable dustbin in a street. I noticed that it was the same street where Mr. Dean first met me. "Should we move out now?" Zhen whispered. "Ah, come on, let's get out of here" I whispered back. We were about to reach the other end of the street until we were confronted by Jon and Stan, the two partners of Mr. Dean. We tried to run back but Mr. Dean was there, standing taller than the gigantic structure of Zhen. "It's time to leave, Kazuo. Thank you for picking up my call that day! Look how time changed both of us! Thanks to you too Zhen...For handing him the phone really cleverly! You deserve equal credit in this robbery!" he said, maintaining the monster laugh scenario, "The only difference is that I got the Murcaxro and you got my bullet". So basically, Zhen handed me the phone deliberately that day. I would have never imagined that the moment I held the phone in my hands, would prove to be so fatal for me. While Mr. Dean was busy with his villainous talks, Zhen turned back and got Stan by his collar. I also closed my eyes and ran towards Jon. The street was abandoned so I didn't expect any help from someone. "Both of you stop! Stop I said!" Mr. Dean cried, but we paid zero attention to the warning though he had a gun in his hand. Zhen got Stan by the neck and threw him in the dustbin. The plantation was so strong; it felt like his bones might have powdered. His eyes closed and then Jon tried to rush me. I got a metal grill in my hand and his abdomen absorbed it. He cried loud. Zhen punched him hard, right on the lips. The momentum between his mouth and Zhen's hand was so powerful that his incisor broke off. He fell to the ground. "You rascal, I'm going to kill you!" Mr. Dean cried, fixed his target on my chest and shoot. I already knew I was dead. A second passed, then another, then another. It doesn't take a bullet 3 seconds to launch from a gun to the target. I was ok so was Mr. Dean. I saw him and he ran away in fear. Was I scary? I saw my shoes then, covered in blood... Down went my eyes and down went Zhen. The bullet had hit him straight in the chest and pierced his heart.

"No!" I cried loud. My heart pounded wildly as I cradled Zhen in my arms, his ashen face a stark contrast against the crimson stain spreading across his torso. "Stay with me, Zhen!" I screamed; panic lacing my voice as I scanned the desolate road for any sign of help. The weight of his body felt lighter with each passing second, but I refused to let despair consume me."Kazuo, I can't..." Zhen's voice was barely a whisper, strained with agony. "Everything will be okay, Zhen, just hold on. Help is coming!" I reassured him, my voice trembling with fear and desperation. I carried his huge body on my shoulder and ran to the main road, trying to get a lift to the City Hospital. Minutes felt like hours until a car pierced through the bad time and screeched to a halt beside us. With trembling hands, I gently laid Zhen in the backseat, his shallow breaths echoing the urgency of our situation. "To the city hospital, please!" I pleaded with the driver, who nodded and sped off under the afternoon light.

The hospital's fluorescent lights flickered overhead as medical staff rushed Zhen into the emergency room. I paced the sterile corridors, my thoughts a whirlwind of guilt and fear. I dialed Mom's number from the reception landline, my voice choked with tears as I recounted the horror that unfolded. Hours dragged on, each minute a silent plea for Zhen's survival. Finally, the doctor emerged, his expression somber. "How is he?" I blurted out before he could utter a word.

"He's lost a lot of blood. We're doing everything we can," the doctor replied, his words hanging heavy in the air. My heart sank, and I could feel the tears threatening to spill over.

"Can I see him?" I asked with a voice, barely audible. Inside the room, Zhen lay pale and weak, but his eyes held a glint of determination. I quietly moved inside.

"Kazuo, listen," he rasped, gripping my hand weakly. "Murcaxro... it's in Naperville, that's all I know"

My mind raced as I tried to absorb his words. "Throw it aside, Zhen, you can't give up. We'll find it together, I promise," I choked out, tears streaming down my face.

He managed a faint smile. "No, you're on your own now... Don't be sorry for me, just take care of Roggy. I just worry about one thing," he said, his mouth half opened. "What's it buddy?" I asked tears still running down. "What if Steve bullies you again? You have some back-up like me? I bet you have not!" he asked and pulled all of his energy in a slight laughter. "Huh, you're right. But I don't need it now. When you get well and we rush to the school, you'll see lot of changes for me. Just get up from this damn bed...You're a fighter, aren't you?" I replied, tears mixing with my smile. "Kazuo, thank you...For everything" Zhen's voice faded, his eyes closing as his hand fell limp.

"Ok, open your eyes now. You can't do this to me! Where did all that Judo and Karate training go? Just wake up, I said!" I pleaded, shaking him gently.

"Kazuo, get up, son," Mom called from behind, tears washing her face as well. She had secretly been hearing to all this. "No, Mom, he is alright, just unconscious!" I consoled her as well as my heart, "He just needs some rest." "But Kazuo" she began, "He's gone".

My head fell on the blood covered chest of Zhen and my eyes cried hard like a baby. The doctor entered and said, "Son, get up…He's gone, we've to take him."

I finally wiped my face. My eyes had turned red, weeping. I still couldn't believe I lost the one who was the most near to me and I realized that he was never going to come back. I kissed Zhen's forehead and hugged him. "Get up now, God will ease everything!" the doctor said. "Oh really! Who did it then!" I pushed his hand away from my shoulder. I didn't want sympathy. I wanted my friend.

Mom tried to lift me up. I removed the oxygen mask from Zhen's face and lifted him in my arms. "Let's get him to the crematoria centre," the doctor said. I moved out of the ICU with Zhen in my arms.

With each step, a tear drop from my eye fell on his face. I, along with some doctors and Mom, reached the crematoria area and I placed Zhen's body into the coffin. For the last time, I kissed him but I didn't wept. I knew what Zhen wanted me to do; stay strong and never give up. As the employees plated the coffin and I would see his face for the last time, I promised him that I would do the same. Each memory of ours, each fight of ours and each mischief of ours just got burned up in the fire as Zhen left forever.

As I started to walk out of the Hospital, the weight of responsibility and loss settled on my shoulders, driving me forward into the unknown. I kicked a piece of already broken glass near the crematoria and shattered it to more pieces. Now I didn't wanted the Murcaxro only! I wanted that freak! I wanted Dean! All I knew was that I was never going to be the same again.

16. SURPRISINGLY BACK

Zhen's last words echoed in my mind. The location of Murcaxro, a painting that held secrets beyond comprehension, hidden by his damn murderer uncle. A legacy left behind, buried in Naperville.

As the evening shadows crept in, I made a decision. I would leave for Naperville tonight, the urgency to uncover the truth overpowering my grief. Ignoring the exhaustion from my previous trip barely some 16 hours ago, I hurriedly packed my bag, memories of Zhen's smiling face haunting every corner of my thoughts. "I am going!" I exclaimed loud enough for Mom to listen. "And may I know to where?" she replied back weakly, still in shock after Zhen's sacrificial death for me. "To Naperville and you won't stop me! Zhen wanted me to do this and I will not let him down," I said bravely. "Who the hell on Earth will stop you?" she replied and came near me. Holding my face in her hands, she said, "Go and do what is important, what is right. Anyone who tries to stop you, crush him!" I could see the ignited fire in her eyes and how vexed she felt.

"I promise Mom!" I replied and left for the station.

The journey back to Naperville was a blur, the wheels of the train clicking rhythmically against the tracks. My mind wandered back to Zhen's revelation. Murcaxro's secret location held the key to millions of dollars and my reputation. How would I come to know where it is in such a far spread place?

Upon reaching Naperville, the darkness of the night enveloped the city. I didn't know what to do? I had neither any relative nor as much money to fetch for a hotel. Only one thought raced through my mind. With determination, I made my way to Mayaan Uncle's house, the memories of our recent encounter still fresh. The warmth of his hospitality despite my earlier debacle at the museum lingered in my mind.

As I approached his door, hesitation gnawed at me. Would he be receptive to my sudden return? Would he understand the urgency that drove me back here?

The door creaked open, revealing Mayaan Uncle's surprised expression. "Kazuo, what brings you here again so soon?" he exclaimed. "Mayaan Uncle, I know it's unexpected, but I need your help," I began, trying to catch my breath from the rush of emotions. "Come in, come in," he gestured, concern etched on his face. We settled in the cozy living room, the antique furniture emitting a sense of comfort amidst my turmoil.

"This afternoon I saw Zhen and he revealed that the painting is here, in Naperville," I explained even after the weight of the words held heavy on my tongue. I thought it was better for me to not tell him about his death. I still couldn't believe it.

Mayaan Uncle's eyes widened in astonishment. The same pale look took over his face just like last night. This reminded me of Zhen's face during his final moments on the ventilator bed. "Zhen, your friend, spoke of Murcaxro? That's... unexpected. But why here?" he barely spoke.

"He said it's hidden by his uncle, Dean," I revealed the urgency palpable in my voice. "Please, I need to find it. We need to finish it now! You know how hard we've been suffering, both of us," I added to the silence.

Mayaan Uncle sighed heavily, his expression shifting from surprise to concern. "I never imagined that this story will take a twist like this. But I trust your judgment, let's do it. You can stay here for as long as you want now! We'll start the search," he said.

He led me through the corridors of his house, the echoes of our footsteps breaking the silence. We reached a locked door, Mayaan Uncle producing a key from his pocket. The room inside was dimly lit, lined with shelves holding various artifacts and paintings.

"This is my private collection," Mayaan Uncle explained, his voice tinged with regret. "I've got all of these since I was young. I'll help you search the

Murcaxro but for now, you need to have some rest" he said and started to walk towards a wooden cupboard.

As I combed through the shelves, my heart raced with anticipation. Each painting held its own story, but one remained elusive. It was a beautiful girl playing a flute. It was like the Murcaxro!

"Uncle, what is this? The Murcaxro is here!" I exclaimed. My tone was a bit low so he didn't notice. I kept watching it and then left towards the corridor again, confused. "I came here to fetch for the keys of the master bedroom. Let's get moving now" Mayaan Uncle said, as he followed me smilingly.

We moved through the long red-carpeted gallery until Mayaan Uncle said first to break the silence, "I hope it doesn't surprise you. I wondered what he was talking about. More than that, I was wondering if that painting was actually the Murcaxro or not? Then, hidden behind a tapestry, a hidden compartment was revealed. Inside rested a faint human structure. He was a man and his ace was enveloped by a black sack. Mayaan uncle moved forward and lifted his 'almost dead' body up. He removed the covering from his head… Dean stood there in his arms, shock and fear painting his face.

"What are you doing here?!" I demanded, my voice quivering.

"Kazuo I didn't mean that, it was an accident" he stammered, caught off guard. I moved forward and punched him hard in the stomach. He fell to the ground and I kicked him. All my frustration came blazing out.

Mayaan Uncle stepped forward and caught me by the waist, "Stop Kazuo! Why are you doing this to him?" he asked. But I kept kicking and replied, "Nothing, he's just a bloody freak. I lost everything because of him!" "Kazuo, stop! I've already tortured him to bad limits. He might die now. Stop I said!" Mayaan Uncle cried. I kicked him twice and the last one drove him straight to unconsciousness. I stopped and calmed myself. "How you got him?" I asked, holding my face. "I found him running today when I came to visit the Police station in Chicago. It's then I caught him. I've been asking him about the painting since afternoon but there was no response from his side," he said and then added, "Why have you beaten him so badly. He might have died!" I sat on a chair and remained silent for 2 minutes. I started weeping. My eyes had already dried up of tears and nothing came out of them now. "Hey Kazuo, tell me son. What is it?" Mayaan Uncle asked with concern. "Uncle..." I stammered, "Zhen is no more. This bastard shot him today. Please allow me to kill him!" I requested. He didn't say anything. The red colored paleness on his face evolved to purple. His eyes spread wide and it felt like he wanted to talk but his tongue had froze. "No! This can't be it! You are joking, right?" he asked half fake-smiling. I felt his arms shivering as he held mine. "Yes it is true!" I replied, tears starting to coast out of my eyes. Mayaan Uncle cried hard. He made himself to the unconscious body of Dean and kicked him thrice hardly on the shin and face. Dean woke up and cried hard as he realized that his shin had fractured. Mayaan Uncle continued crying as well as hitting. I was completely shocked but I didn't say anything. I made up myself, still weeping and asked in confusion, "Uncle, why are you reacting like this. Zhen was my friend. What do you have to do with him?"

Mayaan Uncle stopped punching Dean who was one punch away from death. He held his head in his hands and cried hard. The whole bungalow echoed his cry. He stopped after 15 minutes and kicked Dean again, tears rolling his eyes. "Hey! What happened sir? Please stop! Stop I said!" I scolded. Mayaan uncle cried harder and held my hand in his. "Dean is my brother, unfortunately!" he said, his body totally drained of energy. "What?" I asked. My blood froze. My veins started to tremble. I lost control over my nervous system. "Yes, I don't think you heard my name well. It's Mayaan Denbrough!" he replied. "Wait! You are also a Denbrough? Even Dean and Zhen are also-!" I stopped at the last. "Yes! I told you Dean is my brother! I am Zhen's father Kazuo!" Mayaan Uncle added, crying even harder.

17. A FRIEND INDEED

I didn't say anything. I didn't think anything for the next 10 minutes. I doubt if I was even breathing. All I did was just sitting on the chair nearby, watching Dean's blood covered shirt and Mayaan Uncle crying. I suddenly got up and kicked Dean into the face. His molar broke out and he spitted it on my shoes. He cried in pain. Mayaan Uncle got me by my collar and pushed me back. He lifted Dean on his shoulder and placed him right on a chair. I thought he felt sympathy for him after all that severe beating he put forth. His body was 80% dead. Mayaan Uncle then got his open bottle of hot, boiling coffee and threw it all over Dean's face. He cried in pain. I realized that I was wrong. Well, how can he show sympathy towards a criminal and that too of his own son! Sometime back, if a person was tortured so badly in front of me, I surely would have vomited but after what he did to me and Zhen, it didn't matter that how he was being treated. I better wanted him dead now. His face had turned red and he had blisters on it. Mayaan Uncle got a 6-bullet revolver and was about to shoot him when I screamed, "NO! Don't do this sir or we would never know where the painting is!" he dropped his gun for a second and then shot Dean twice in the leg. I screamed. Mayaan Uncle had totally lost it. "There is not a damn thing he can tell you about the painting, you understand!" he cried, red eyed and shot him straight in the head. The shoot of the bullet wasn't strong enough for anyone to listen and also, his house was isolated in the thin bushes and tall trees of Naperville. His house was the last and house no. 14, the predecessor one, was somewhat 1 km away. I was helpless and hopeless. I believed that it was my turn next. I simply stared Dean's dead body without any blink. I couldn't believe I had seen two deaths because of me in less than 36 hours, although I was happy for this one. Mayaan Uncle left the room. He returned within a couple of seconds and handed me a canvas. It was the Murcaxro I saw in his master gallery. Was it really it? "Uncle, what is this?" I asked as if I didn't know. "Murcaxro!" he replied and started pushing me out of the room and his house. On the way I asked him a zillion questions but he didn't reply any of them and we kept going. I was shocked, relieved and confused at the same time. I walked to the station and left for my home.

I reached Chicago at around 8:00 PM in the evening and walked to my home, though I had enough money to go for a cab as well. I asked myself questions and self-answered them but I think my life was almost back in my grip.

After 45 minutes, I was at the footsteps of my apartments and I saw a lady sitting there. She was Mom. She rushed to me and hugged me. I hugged her back. "So, you found anything?" she asked, stammering. "Huh, I got the painting but not the answers I wanted" I replied. "Seriously, thank God Kazuo! Finally, we can get back!" she said with a wide smile on her face. I could see the tears in her eyes, ready to fall anytime. "Of course Mom but there are still some questions hanging in my mind. What about them?" I asked. "No! Just cut it short here. You aren't going for any answers or justifications now Kazuo. What you actually were in search for, you got it!" she replied immediately and started weeping. I held her head against my chest and requested her to be calm as life was normal again, and to be honest, everyone walking by was watching us. I was not confident on my earlier statement. At what cost did I have my life back on track? My only childhood friend, Zhen? There is one more but I better not talk about him. In fact, I should try to forget him. All of this drama was just because of him and he suffered his deserving faith. I had unimaginable number of questions roaming in my head but this was not the right time. I helped Mom to walk the stairs up to our apartments. We entered inside and I made her sit on the couch. As she stopped weeping, I got her a lukewarm glass of water. She held my hand for the next 30 minutes until I realized that she had fallen asleep. I carefully released my hand from her grip because I didn't want her to wake up. She deserved a good nap. I got control of the kitchen and made myself a small dinner. I knew that Mom was only waiting for me as she neither had made dinner nor washed the dishes. After I was done,

I took a look at her. She was looking innocent as always. I got her and myself a blanket. She slept peacefully on the couch and I slept by her side on the floor, staring the roof of the lobby for an hour. Then I reached my bag and got the Murcaxro. It had something in it which made robbers and lovers fall for it. But how did Mayaan Uncle have it? It was shocking to know that he was Zhen's father. Then why did Zhen live alone since childhood if he had his father alive? Was he not aware of this fact? Or did Mayaan Uncle kick him out of his house for any reason? A wave of curiosity took over my brain. I thought it was better for me to give it some rest. I put the Murcaxro back in the hiking bag and placed it above my cupboard in my room. I got back in the blanket and slept in heavens. Everything was normal and no more secrets were to be revealed now, I guess.

As I woke up, the wall clock was against my time schedule. It showed 7 O' clock in the morning. I was going to be late as always. Mom was still sleeping and I didn't pardon her. I quickly did all I could in the next 1 hour and at sharp 8 O' clock, I was down at the footsteps of the stairs, waiting for my bus. I had left a message for Mom on the landline and closed the door from outside. As the bus arrived, I tried to look normal so that no one could notice that I had seen two murders in two days.

As I entered, I gave out a really huge grin and everyone stared at me. It has only been some days since my new image was born in the school but I realize that they were treating me right before. I am always doing such non-sensible things around which make everyone call me Mr. Weirdo. Like, what was the use of giving such a dirty and scary smile? Ashamed of my action, I sat quietly on the front seat and looked out of the window, trying to make everyone forget about what just happened 10 seconds before. I was lost in my own world of imagination until we reached school. I walked 22 steps and then felt a hand on my shoulder. It was Steve's. I only smiled at this action of his until he said first, "We all feel sorry to know that he has left for a more peaceful place. May his soul rest in peace!" I suddenly realized that Zhen was not there in the school today and he was never going to be. My only support, outside my home, was Zhen and now that he is gone, I was left alone forever. Steve's gang arrived on the scene and showed sympathy to me. I didn't know if they had attended his funeral or not as I was swimming in a black hole at that time. "Thanks guys! It was what God wanted to happen but we'll always have Zhen around us and in us, right?" I replied and all others nodded. I attended all the classes quietly and somehow, peacefully. During the recess, I was in the canteen, having my lunch. I watched a news channel on the television which the canteen head was watching since morning. "Uncle, are you going to change it or not? You've been watching this channel since the school was constructed!" I demanded. He was about to change it until a news emerged on the screen under the bold title of BREAKING NEWS!

Senior Official from the Police Department, Naperville, Mr. Mayaan Denbrough arrested under the charge of a murder of his own brother. Police officials found the dead body in the basement of his house this morning and he is being taken to the jail in Naperville for death as his punishment tomorrow morning. The case is still going under investigation.

The water bottle in my hand dropped to the floor and it was all hell there. I couldn't react. I couldn't lift my spoon. All I did was only sit there and listen to the news again and again for clarity. I jumped from the 4-seater bench, left the hot doughnut waiting there, rushed into the librarian's chamber and requested her to write me a Half-day leave application to the Principal. She could see the tension on my face and thus, granted my request. I kept the application on the Principal's table as he was out for a round. I left the school premises and ran to my home which was 7 kilometers away. As expected, it was a useless idea as the heavy load of my bag buried my shoulders. I showed hand to a private car and luckily, it stopped by my side. "Thank you sir!" I exclaimed with no expression as I seated in the car. "Is everything ok buddy? You look worried about something" the young boy asked with compassion. "Oh yeah, I am good. Just leaving for some urgency!" I lied. He drove the car as fast as he could and asked me irrelevant questions on the way. I simply nodded and replied with a 'huh' in short but he couldn't understand that I was ignoring him. Well, that is not like me usually but this time, I was going mad from the inside. How did the police get to know that Mayaan Uncle had killed Dean?

"Oh thanks sir. Please stop here" I said as the car reached my place. "It's ok pal. Take care!" he replied and left. I ran faster than a thunderbolt and within few seconds, I was at the main door, ringing the bell with an angry finger. "Kazuo, what brings you home so early today?" Mom asked as I entered and started packing my bag. "I'll narrate the whole story to you later. I immediately have to leave for Naperville right now! I have enough money to fetch for the ticket from here but not enough for the return ticket. Can you please borrow me 20$?" I said in a single breath. "But dear, what do you have to do in Naperville. You got the stolen painting, right. That's it!" she asked confusingly. "Not for that Mom. Mayaan Uncle is arrested and punished with death! I have to meet him before something terrible happens" I replied quickly. "But what has he done? Is he himself not a police officer?" she asked questions after questions. "Mom, Mr. Dean is his brother. He killed him yesterday!" I replied in short. Mom looked at me with fear. She cried at me and said, "So what actually happened yesterday? Tell me everything!" I made my way to her bag in her room and took 20$ from it myself. I ran back to the lobby and wore my casual shoes. She kept asking questions, trying to stop me but I was determined. I made my way to the staircase and she followed me till the last stair. Finally, frustrated, I replied all her questions with a single answer, "This is not the best time Mom. I'll tell you everything but right away, I need to go. Mayaan Uncle has helped me a lot; it's my turn to pay back."

18. LESSON LEARNT; DON'T TRY TO BE A HERO!

She didn't say anything and that meant she allowed me to go. I ran as fast as I could. There was no time for a cab. As expected, my chest started to pain. I still kept running and surprisingly, I was at the station within an hour, after a harsh marathon race all over Chicago. I made my way inside and luckily, there was no crowd or line of human beings so far. As I bought myself a ticket, the announcement speakers hit hard in my ear drums. "The 4th metro to Naperville about to leave in 5 minutes", the announcer said. I rushed to the platform and in the train. As I entered, the door closed behind me. I was really lucky enough! The journey back to Naperville for the third time was a complete mess. I kept standing for half an hour until I got a seat next to the door grill. I was lost in the thoughts of Mayaan Uncle and how he shaped my life, from horrible to normal to horrible again. As the train geared down, I was sure that I was in Naperville. The smell of the mustard fields made it more relevant to me more than anything. I left the dreadful station and walked through the graveyard cum roads of Naperville. Everything seemed lifeless.

As I reached Mayaan Uncle's house, it was all wrapped in police investigation. Nobody was allowed to enter or leave the place. The police officers had dark circles under their eyes which meant they didn't have quiet of a night. It was scary all around. I was not a lot known to Naperville other than the road from the Railway station to Mayaan Uncle's house. How will I find him then? As I left the crime scene, I wondered 'Where the lifeless body of Dean might be?' I walked slowly and slowly. After 10 minutes I found a Police officer, changing the back space of his Police car. I, without any hesitation, asked him, "Ah, sir? Do you know where Mr. Mayaan Denbrough, the man who has a murder charge on him is?" the man looked straight in my eyes and asked me back, "Are you his relative or what?" I was sure he would shoot me at the centre of my head if I said anything related to the episode yesterday. "No, I am his friend. Just heard about the incident and decided to have a look at him!" I replied. He smiled and I relieved. Then he said, "Friend? You are too young to be called a friend of an old and harsh Police officer! I am Paul, one of Mayaan sir's disciples. He has been teaching me since 5 years but heart sinks thinking of what he has done!" It was my lucky day. I was hoping that this guy could help me in meeting Mayaan Uncle. Without wasting seconds, I asked him again, "Sir, can you please help me? I am stuck as I am new here. Can you please tell me where is he taken to? It is very urgent for me to meet him!" There was a reflection of curiosity in his eyes. Now I was worried if he really could do something or not? "Alright little bro, let me see" he replied after a good thinking. Then he continued doing his work with the car and as he was done, he told me to sit in. I did as he directed. He drove the car all over Naperville and I was left hanging in frustration.

"Sir, how long is it going to take?" I finally asked. "Just few more minutes" he replied with ease, ignoring the fact that I was about to jump out. I had millions of questions hanging in my cerebellum and I wanted Mayaan Uncle to answer each one of them, clearly! As I was usually lost in my world, the guy shook me. "Wake up buddy! We are here!" he exclaimed. I just sat in the car and he went to the jailer's compartment and asked him for permission. It was really a tough job to get a permission granted for a prisoner who is being taken for hanging tomorrow morning. I wish I could wake up, thinking all this was just a nightmare but no, it wasn't. This was reality and it had consequences. Officer Paul came rushing to the car and said, "Hurry up kiddo! He granted only 30 minutes for the meeting!" I jumped out of the car and thanked him. We rushed to the cell he was kept in and it is then I saw his 'maybe' generous soul wandering in the prison cell, waiting for Death's grim scythe. I called him first, "Sir...Uncle...I am here." he stood up in surprise and almost came forward, either to hug me or slap me but then he stopped. "You should not be here!" he whispered. "And neither should you!" I cried. "No boy. I deserved this. Whatever I've done, good or bad, law has no sight of mercy or kindness for it. A crime is a crime!" he replied, his voice full of regret.

The air in the cell hung heavy, not just with institutional disinfectant but with unspoken grief. Officer Paul, the Police officer and disciple of Mayaan Uncle, who'd facilitated this crazy meeting, stood awkwardly a few paces back, silent sentinel in a starched uniform. Across the chipped metal table sat Mayaan Uncle, the man who'd become a legend, a monster, and now, just...Mayaan Uncle.

His face, usually etched with lines of authority, was a mask of exhaustion. His eyes, the same deep as mine, were dull. He wore the standard-issue orange jumpsuit, the vibrant color a stark contrast to his faded spirit. Shame gnawed at me. Shame for everything –for stealing the painting only and only for bad, for my best friend's death, for Mayaan Uncle's actions and for even being here.

"Mayaan Uncle," I started, my voice cracking. "I don't..." I trailed off, unsure how to begin.

He let out a ragged sigh and said, "Don't pretend, Kazuo. You know why you're here."

His bluntness stung, but it cleared the head fog of emotion. "Yes. I came to help…" I began. I didn't want Paul to listen any of our conversation except for the helping part. Thus, I reached across the table, my hand hovering an inch away from his. He didn't flinch.

"Help?" he snorted a humorless sound, "You can't help, boy. Not anymore."

"There's still time. Officer Paul has connections, I guess… And anyhow, I can get you out of here. I am not sure if he'll help but he says that he has been your disciple, so I think…" I stopped for him to understand.

Mayaan Uncle's gaze turned steely. "Don't waste your breath. The noose waits, and it waits deservedly," he said.

His words hit me like a physical blow. "But...why? Why Dean? And if he was your brother, then why you didn't arrest him or something earlier? I mean you know what happened and now I know that you knew it as well! Ah! What is this story revolving around? I am sure you know something so don't try to lie!" I exclaimed loud and frustated.

He leaned forward, his voice dropping to a low growl. "He wasn't the man you thought he was, Kazuo. He was a viper, he killed my son and he got you to steal the painting. He deserved this but there is something more. I don't think it is all Dean's or even Zhen's fault at an instance!" he stopped.

"Deserved? I don't care about anything else! You are Zhen's father, alright. You are Dean's brother, alright. I might have trust issues with you as well now, alright. But you can't be judge, jury, and executioner!" I echoed, incredulous. Anger flared, but a chilling realization dawned. "Did he know about my Dad?" I added. A flicker of pain crossed his face, fleeting but undeniable. "It doesn't matter now" he said.

"It does!" I slammed my fist on the table, the metal clanging. "It matters because it explains everything. But it doesn't excuse it!" I finished my speech.

Silence stretched between us, thick with unspoken truths. The clock on the wall ticked, each second a hammer blow against my dwindling hope.

Mayaan Uncle finally spoke, his voice hoarse. "Leave, Kazuo. Go mourn your Dean and Dad and live your life. Don't waste it on a lost soul like me. Let me mourn for my son for the last few hours of my life." His words stung, but a sliver of understanding bloomed amidst the anger. It wasn't just about Dean, was it? I hated him more than anything. It was about a past stained with pain, about choices that had brought him to this grim cell.

He wasn't just Mayaan Uncle, the respected policeman. He was a man consumed by vengeance, clinging to a twisted sense of justice. My heart went out to him, a surge of sympathy battling with the anger simmering within. Just then, Officer Paul cleared his throat. "Time's up, buddy. Time's up sir. We have to leave now"

Thirty minutes was all we had. I had millions of questions but watching him, I thought of better not asking them. Maybe I couldn't stop the hanging and maybe he deserved this. I can't get him out of here.

As I was about to leave, he began, holding my hand, "Kazuo, wait! I have something to tell you."

"But sir, we are out of time. Who is answerable to the management then?" Paul argued. "No! This is important stuff and when I die tomorrow, I am going to regret in hell that I didn't confess you this guilt of mine!" he replied, red-eyed.

Well another confession…Ahhh! I don't have enough left to hear more secrets.

19. ENIGMA REVEALED!

"We were long time friends" he began. "Who uncle?" I asked empathically. "Your dad and me" he closed his mouth and I opened mine. "What, how do you know him? I mean I just know you since some days only and we met accidently. How do you know my Dad? How?!" I asked. My arms had turned red. I had goose bumps as hard as brick. "Yes dear. Your dad and I met at the National Art Academy. He was the greatest artist present around there. Finally it all changed when..." he stopped. "When what, sir? When what?" I asked, not letting him breath. "When The Grand National Canvas Competition showed up and he conquered all! His masterpiece was held in the State Museum as to give due respect but it enraged the inner, teen-self of mine. I was jealous!" he stammered. I couldn't believe what I just heard. Mayaan Uncle first being my friend's father, then my father's friend and then getting jealous of his achievement! That's ridiculous! "Time's up buddy. We really need to go or the consequences will be harsh...!"Officer Paul spoke for the first time after 10 minutes. "No! Not now sir, I've got to know more about this!" I replied in an aggressive manner. "Kazuo, it was entirely my fault. I bought Zhen a bungalow in the outskirts of Chicago. Kept him out of my sight for years and when I found him, he was not able to speak. He had gone for a better place! I was waiting for the best time and then I persuaded Dean to persuade you for the robbery of the same painting of your Dad, only so that I could burn it to ashes. He lied every time to you but only on my directions. Even yesterday's episode, me telling you that I caught Dean while I was in Chicago was a part of the plan until you informed me about the killing of my son!" he said in a single breath, tears rolling down his eyes. I was shocked from the inside but from the outside, it was no big deal now for me to hear some new and old, unveiling enigmas. "Good!" I said and started to get up, leaving then cell. "I am sorry Kazuo! I am the criminal for the city but I don't give a damn to it. I am your criminal and for that, you are all allowed to kill me right here!" he said. "Ok pal, you have get out of here!" Officer Paul roared as he thought I would really do something like that. I crossed over the huge table and got myself right in front of Mayaan Uncle. I leaned forward and hugged him tight. Both of us cried loud enough for everybody else to listen. I wiped my tears and realized that it was all on track now but still, I won't be able to help him. Even the hope of Officer Paul doing something was shattered to the ground. I'll take your leave now sir! I know it is too late but it was an honor, doing anything or even something with you. It was really adventurous!" I replied with a fake smile. "Goodbye dear. God bless you. I know I've done something which will ever be engraved in your heart, but hopefully, you'll remember your Dad through this or maybe…me also" he replied, wiping his eyes. We finally gave out a hug again and I started walking out of the cell, followed by Officer Paul. The corridors went brighter and brighter and Mayaan Uncle's smile, dimmer and dimmer. I left the jail and never looked back for the rest of the path. Officer Paul drove the car straight to the station on my request and didn't say a single thing on the way. On reaching, I thanked Officer Paul as he left. I stared the skyscrapers for a minute and then promised myself never to look back at Naperville again. I boarded the train and after 1 hour and 30 minutes, I was backing home.

As I reached my place and knocked at the door, there was a sense of satisfaction as well as dissatisfaction in my voice. I was satisfied that it had all ended now and I can go back to my normal routine. On the other hand, dissatisfaction engulfed me as I would never be able to see Mayaan Uncle and especially Zhen, now in my whole lifetime. I looked down at my dust covered boots. I looked back at the flashback of this story and then made a decision. I was just thinking until Mom opened the door and held me tight. "You are home, my dear! Are you tired?" she asked passionately. "No, I am good. Where is the Murcaxro?" I asked. "It's in the drawer of my room. Why are you asking?" she exclaimed. "I need it right now!" I emphasized. "But why do you need it now? I mean, you can give it to the authorities tomorrow as well!" she replied. "No authorities. Just hand it over to me" I replied. "Alright!" she said and got me the painting. I held the painting tight in my hands and left for my room. I got a hammer and two nails along and struck them tight with one blow. Then I hung the Murcaxro on the wall besides my bed. "Why are you doing this Kazuo? Don't you have to give it back?" Mom asked. "Oh, giving it back! Well at what cost Mom? At the cost of my father, my friend or Mayaan Uncle? This painting right here was made by Dad and we deserve it, not those so called 'authorities' of the Museum!" I replied aggresively. "Dear, you don't understand. What happens when they are not able to find the Murcaxro any time in future? All doubts are on you then, right?" Mom said, debating. "I don't care whether they find it or not. Mayaan Uncle already gave my justification that day in the Museum, so no more inquiries and no more dramas. I am having this!" I replied, adrenaline rushing in my soul. "Ok...Ok Kazuo, you can have it. Maybe, you are right. This right here is made by your Dad and we deserve it more than anything!" she said and kissed me on the forehead. I hugged her and said, "I love you Mom!"

Then we had our dinner and I made it quick to my bed. After a long time it felt as if Dad was sleeping by my side when I was about to get in my bed. The excitement was such that I kept waking up every 1 hour. Finally I slept peacefully around 4:30 AM in the morning and woke around 6:00 AM. The Murcaxro was still hanging as kept yesterday.

Mom rushed in my room with the same mug of coffee as always and said, "There you go. You didn't have quite of a night, right?" I looked up to her and then to the mirror on the side-table. I had minor dark-circles under my eyes. "Yes, I think so!" I replied pointing to my eyes and we both laughed. "Ok get yourself ready or you'll be late for school!" she said, leaving my room. After I was done having a heavy bath, only to remove the smell I was carrying from Naperville, I moved out in my towel only and saw the painting, leaning a bit. I got it and placed it back in the same position. The girl playing the flute in the canvas looked more beautiful than anything. The painting will remind me of the adventure, the ups and downs I had this month and which were left residing in my heart forever. I came to know about a very moral lesson for my entire life. Though responsibilities shoulder us sometimes, but we should never go with what is basically wrong in fulfilling them and that is what Dad, Zhen and Mayaan Uncle taught me respectively. I walked up to my window to breathe some fresh air until Mom cried, "Aren't you done yet Kazuo? You are going to be late!" I looked down at the street and found my bus rushing to the foot stairs of my apartment. "Oh crap! Mom, I am late!" I cried. I dressed up as quickly as possible and stitched the bread between my jaws that Mom handed me. I rushed down the staircase and made them noise for rest of the neighbors to know that Mr. Kazuo Tanaka was late as usual. I was late by 4 minutes and the bus driver was almost half asleep on the steering. "Uncle, let's go!" I screamed my voice full of confidence. I didn't care what everyone else would think. I was proud that the most wanted and forgot painting of the city was hanging in my room. The museum officials were showing no action in response to the robbery of the Murcaxro so I was calm. They will never ever get me on the line, all thanks to Mayaan Uncle. He might be taken to the noose long back this morning. I missed him, though he held equal fault in this tragedy. As I reached school, I felt that something was different. There was a hand on my shoulder and the person there was cracking jokes and laughing with himself. After $1/30^{th}$ of a second, I realized that he was Steve. "How are you, friend?" I asked with a smiling face. I would have never imagined that I will call Steve 'friend'! "I am ok Kaz! See you in the class!" he replied with the same face. He shortening my name was unexpected as well and I felt that yes, I had a backup building now.

Our first class was Art & Craft and our teacher was recently changed. He was Mr. Yamada, an old but spiritual Japanese artist. Our school had got extra expenses to get him from Japan. Each one of the students was given a canvas until he spoke in an Anglo-Japanese tone, "Students, you're given 40 minutes for the painting. Move your brushes and paint something which has turned your life in any manner, deep within which spirituality resides!" Every student was doing his job with full concentration except for me. I just watched the birds outside on the trees, building a nest until I realized that only 10 minutes were left. Yet I painted slowly and finally my masterpiece was ready. I had no intention painting this but my hands automatically did the job. Maybe, my sub-conscious helped them. I smiled at the work and kissed it. Mr. Yamada came to every student's desk and watched the canvas carefully, unsatisfied! He finally approached me. "So dear, show me your art!" he asked. Proudly lifting my eye-brows, I showed him. "What? You've painted a phone!" he giggled. I smiled and said, "Sir, though you might not see any spirituality in this but you know what, a phone call can change one's life!"

www.ingramcontent.com/pod-product-compliance
Lightning Source LLC
LaVergne TN
LVHW041531070526
838199LV00046B/1617